The Motions

By Kristal Moon

Dedication

To my sister, Adriene, who constantly introduces to
some and reminds others of who "the writer" is
when mentioning my name!

Prologue

I tapped my nails nervously against the desk. The silence in the motel room was thick with tension. The curtains in the small but quaint room were closed tightly, overlapping each other to guarantee total privacy from the passersby outside. It was raining hard. You could almost hear every drop as it plunged toward the earth. It had been so nice earlier in the day; the sun was out and the weather was just right. As soon as I pulled into the parking lot of the motel, the clouds seemed to come from out of nowhere. In an instant, it became dark and started to rain big, huge drops.

I made a mad dash to the door and knocked furiously. In the five seconds it took for me to get to the door, I was soaked! Now I was sitting in this room, dripping wet while my clothes stuck to me and my hair plastered to my head, wondering if I still had a future with the only man I had ever loved. I looked over at Reggie; his big, brown eyes mirrored the sadness in his voice as he spoke.

"Look, baby I know things have really been a mess between us, but I wanna make them better."

"So just like that, you wanna get back together?" I asked him.

Reggie walked over to me and dropped to both knees.

"Well I don't expect it to be easy, but I'd like to try."

I didn't want to, but I couldn't help looking into those dark brown eyes of his. I used to love gazing into them, trying to figure out what was behind them; what they were trying to say when his mouth could not form the words. Plus, his long and full eyelashes made me absolutely weak!

"Karena," he whispered. "I love you to the third degree. I want you to be my wife, for me to be your husband. We've been through so much and it took me some time to get my head straight, but I'm in love with you; and I know you still love me!"

I couldn't stand it anymore. I got up and walked over to the bed. That was a big mistake! As soon as I sat down on the soft, king size bed, I began imaging us making love and how good it would feel. It would feel even better this time because my body was incredibly tense and nobody knew how to work it like Reggie; that I could not even lie about!

I wondered what got us here, what it was that caused us to get to this point. All the plans were made; we were going to get married, have children, and live happily ever after. But I should have known better. That shit only happens in the movies!

"I know that you love me and of course I still love you", I told him. "But we haven't been together for a while. And if we do work things out I don't want our past coming back to haunt us."

Now, I did not look directly at him while I was talking, but I could feel his eyes practically burning a hole through my chest. I breathed heavily, not knowing what was going to come next. I closed my eyes and after what seemed like an eternity, I opened them realizing they were filling up with tears. I hated feeling like this, so sensitive and vulnerable. I especially hated Reggie seeing me like this. I never was the type to show my feelings to others. I guess that was one of those funny little quirks about me.

Reggie looked defeated. Everything in his demeanor told me so; his shrunken shoulders, the pleading look in his watery eyes, and the way his quick breaths seemed to stop suddenly.

"So is this it for us, Karena? Are you officially letting me go? After all this time, you're giving up on me, on us?" Reggie asked.

. Struggling, I managed to look at him. I got all these flashbacks, like the first time we met and the first time we made love. We were happy. We did things that normal, monogamous couples did, like play miniature golf and go to carnivals and plays. We held hands and walked in the park, had couple's night out with our friends, and drank and played cards together. I used to rest my head on his shoulder and he would gently run his slender fingers across my cheek. I felt secure, wanted, and most of all, loved. I wanted to forget this whole madness and run into his arms, leaving the past behind.

But my doubts were still looming over me and enabled me from doing so. I couldn't lie and pretend everything was cool, that things would work out fine. My heart was officially broken and my pride would not let me forget that.

"I just don't know how we could keep this relationship together. I'm at the end of my rope and I don't think I can hang on much longer."

.

Karena

(One year earlier)

"Let me give it to you, baby!"

Mannie roared in a deep voice. He raised both of my legs higher in the air and pushed himself deeper inside me. As he pushed and pumped his way to sexual satisfaction, I laid there, damn near motionless wondering what the hell I was doing there in the first place. There I was hanging halfway off a bed with no fitted sheet on it, just one that had been thrown over the mattress, with Mannie's medium-size frame crumpled on top of me.

The upside-down angle I had of the bedroom allowed me to see the chipped paint on the ceiling along with a few wads of chewing gum that had been hurled at it. I shuddered, thinking about how long it might have been up there. Mannie must have thought I was feeling him because he shouted, "Yeah, that's right, this is my pussy!" I wanted to bust out laughing, but I maintained my composure, hoping he would finish soon.

Back to the room: the carpeting was that brown, shaggy kind, you know, from the seventies. The walls looked like they might have been a creamy white color, back in the day! Now, it was covered with a dirty film that made it look beige. Let's not even talk about the curtains, or shall I say, the sheets that were being paraded as curtains. They should have been on the damn bed, not hanging up by a pair of rusty thumbtacks! I know that some guys are dirty, that's to be expected. However, homeboy was downright ridiculous! He had pizza boxes and beer bottles all over the room, and this is *after* I told him he had to pick up a bit before I let him touch me, since I almost broke my neck when I tripped over an empty six-pack box on my last visit.

I know you must be thinking, *what the hell is she doin' messin' around with such a fool anyway?* The answer to that question is his tongue!

Mannie was cute, don't get me wrong. He was a warm caramel color with black, curly hair that brought out his brown eyes. He had a nice personality, a job, and though it did not pay much, it was still work. However, his tongue made me want to scream!

He knew the precise way to eat me out, too. He would go slow in the beginning, then speed it up after a few licks. Just as I would be about to cum, he would slow down and tease me for a while. I loved every minute of it! He was not too bad in the dick department either. Up until I met him, I had never known a guy who could stay erect and keep going after *two* orgasms! I am not the type to run away from the dick, especially when it's good, but I had to tell him to stop a few times because I just couldn't keep up!

So you see, even though Mannie was cool, it was the sex that kept me in his graces. It was usually so good, which is why I could not understand my inability to enjoy it this time, much less climax. I must admit, as turned off as I was, I did feel a little bad. Mannie was working hard to get me in the mood. But today, it just wasn't enough.

"You feel it baby?" He asked, huffing and puffing. "You feel that dick inside you, don't you? I know it feels good!"

Well after that he must have lost his damn mind because all of a sudden he yelled, "Say my name, Karena! What's my name? Whose is it?"

That does it!

I could take no more. I pushed him off me, jumped up from the bed, and began putting my clothes back on. He gave me a confused look as he kneeled on the bed, his hard manhood exposed.

"Karena, baby what's wrong?"

"Look, Mannie this isn't working for me", I told him. "I'm just not in the mood today, I guess." I knew he would try to talk me out of leaving, but I continued to get dressed.

"I wasn't working it enough for you?" He asked pitifully as he wrapped a towel around his waist. "What, do you want me to eat your pussy some more? You know I don't mind; I always want to please you."

I pondered that for a moment. Hey, I cannot help it if the boy got skills in the tongue department! We could have one last lick-me-low session, for old time's sake. However, as I looked at him staring at me like a sick puppy and glanced once more at his hideous room, I knew this was the end of the road.

I told him, "as tempting as that sounds, I'ma have to pass. You know I like the way you handle yourself in the bedroom, but I think this is over. I don't need a fuck friend, Mannie." I gathered the rest of my belongings and headed for the door. Just as I was about to leave, he grabbed my arm.

"But I can be your man; I can take care of you. I've been tryin' to make this thing official for a long time now."

That time, I could not help myself. I cracked up laughing right there and shut the door in his face.

The night air was crisp and cool, a rarity for Columbus in the summertime. I promise you, it seems like the sun just sits only over Ohio. I know that's crazy, but it can get hot as hell here!

I sped through downtown at about eighty miles an hour, the wind whipping my hair all around. I loved cruisin' around the city, especially at night. That is when everything jumped off and you were bound to see cars stuffed with people on their way to whatever club or hotspot; just out to kick it and have a good time. I loved it even more when there was no traffic. I absolutely hated traffic, so please believe that I have road rage! Not the crazy kind, where I would follow someone home after they cut in front of me, but I will not say that I have never been tempted, that's for sure!

Once I got home, I took a long bath, blasted Lauren Hill and thought about my life. I always got a little philosophical whenever I listened to her, she made me actually sit back and think about things, try to gain a little perspective. I felt like something was missing, like there was something I was supposed to have or be doing. I had gone to college, for a while at least, and I was working an okay enough job. But I was never the type to settle for less than the best, and to be honest, lately that's all I had been doing.

As I was putting on my blue cotton pajamas, I looked at myself in the mirror. I am not a cocky young woman, but I did think I was attractive. My dark skin was smooth and flawless. My lips were thick, not too much, and what I thought to be my sexiest physical asset. I always wore my hair in micros braids because I hated doing it and that style was so cute. I was a bit on the full figured size; my dark brown eyes were slanted, and seemed to disappear when I smiled.

The phone rang and when I checked the caller I.D. I saw that it was Mannie.

"Of course", I said aloud. I did not feel like talking to him so I let the call roll over to voicemail.

Mannie was not a bad person; he just wasn't boyfriend material to me. He wanted to try to make me fall in love with him and always brought up the subject of us getting together on a more emotional level. I do not mind being in relationships, they can be kinda fun in fact. But I refuse to fall in love. When the L word comes in to the game, I stop playing.

I have never been in love or even told a guy I loved him. I never had the chance because they always did something stupid to mess things up before I could go there, even if they had already said the words to me. Besides, almost every woman I know who has ever claimed to be in love has always ended up getting hurt, with the exception of my mom.

I am not the type to sit and cry over a man. Nobody wants to be hurt and I be damned if I give my heart to a man then he goes and breaks it! No thanks, that's why I always get out of the loop before a guy even has that chance. Who needs love anyway?

I guess now you must be thinking that I had some kind of really messed up childhood or something, like my family didn't love or take care of me and that's why I feel the way I do. That is not the case. I had a very great upbringing and my parents spoiled me rotten.

I was a cubby girl with a moist Jeri curl and red-framed glasses (can you believe my mom for letting me walk around like that?), but I was still a cutie! My outfits always matched from head to toe and were ironed to perfection. When I got a little older, my mom got the hint and let me trade my greasy curl for braids, thank God!

I was raised in a hand-clappin', foot stompin', tongue talkin', Pentecostal church of God in Christ. Sang in every choir from the Sunshine Band (the kiddie choir) to the young adult one, was in almost every play, and served on the usher board for over seven years! Like most of the "saints", (you know who I'm talkin' 'bout!) I caught religion on Sunday but let it go come Monday morning. Hallelujah anyhow.

My parents are somewhat traditional; my mom is truly a woman of God and my dad is a hardworking, blue-collar man with calluses on his hands. It was my mom who made sure my older brother, sister, and I went to church and participated. I am the baby of the bunch and every bit the spoiled-rotten brat you could imagine, and then some!

You would think that after all the church I have encountered I would be quite the angel, right? Truthfully, I am a sweetheart, but I was quite the demon child back in the day I have to admit! Once I started getting into boys, honey, my parents wanted to throw me into a home for heathens and throw away the key! I was not a hot ass or anything; don't get me wrong, I've just always been a big flirt.

Fast-forward several years and boyfriends later and here I am; twenty-two, still living with my parents, working a crappy collections job for a credit card company and I mean to tell you, I was getting sick to death of being in these going-nowhere-fast types of relationships. At the most they last about six months and I always end up coming out of them feeling as unfulfilled as I did going into them. Nine times out of ten, I would be the one giving, never receiving. I have to say; I am a good woman! I take care of my man, when I have one.

Before I started messing around with Mannie, I was talking to this guy named Kevin for a while. I liked the way our names flowed together: Karena and Kevin. Anyway, he was a thirty year old virgin and when he first told me that, I thought he was lyin'! I mean c'mon, how many men do you know that are virgins, especially past their twenties?

Kevin was nice, always opened doors for me and paid for everything when we would go out, even if I offered to. He had a good job, a nice car, and an amazing personality. I thought to myself,

"Now maybe this can go somewhere". I was wrong!

Everyone knows that first dates are merely interviews: What do you like to do for fun? Where do you work? What kind of music do you like, etc.? The first few months are the getting-to-know-each-other stage. But best believe, give it about three months and that's when people started to show their asses! You begin to notices things, little things at first. Then all hell begins to break loose!

I would often ask Kevin why he waited so long to have sex. I knew he was not the holy type, he wasn't ugly, and he didn't seem to be too shy. He said it was because he studied too hard in school to have time to date, and no girl really took an interest in him. When he expressed interest in hooking up with me on a sexual level, the thought of breakin' in a man his age pumped my head up a bit. I had tricks and positions I could not wait to put on him!

The night we were going to do our thang I made sure I was looking good and smelling even better. He was a tall dude, so I figured he would have a nice package. My mistake! As I felt around his trousers, I noticed that his dick was not much bigger than one of my fingers, minus my acrylic nail!

It took me forever to coax him into eating my pussy and when he finally got down there, he was kissin' and licking it like he was scared to find out what flavor it was. What's worse is he would only do it in the missionary position; I could hardly feel a thing!

After all that, his head got a little big. He stopped being so sweet and he wanted to do it every time we saw each other. After a few months, he told me that he loved me. I pretended as if I was too overwhelmed to speak at the moment. The next day we were talking on the phone and my line beeped. I told him I would call him back, but I never did. I had to let him go!

Before Kevin, there was Daron. Now he was from the Bahamas originally, but had grown up in the states. He still had a slight accent that drove me bananas, and he was sexy as hell! He had a real muscular build, creamy cocoa skin, and a dick to die for! *He* had no trouble eating me out and flipped my body in so many directions, I thought he was gonna break me! But of course, he too had to show his ass after promising me the world. What a crock! I could have stayed with him for the sex, that was reason enough, but he moved away to Philly and that was that.

I cannot even tell you how many others there were; boyfriends or ones that was just tryin to get some.

My longest relationship was with Erick, he lasted a little over a year. We met at a party and after that, we talked on the phone every day, mostly about nothing. I was in high school and you know how high school kids are; they can just sit and breathe on the phone as long as the one they "love" is on the other end.

Erick did not start to show his ass until *after* it had been a long time. He got a little too comfortable and began to treat me like his mother instead of his woman.

He wanted me to cook dinner at my house, and then bring it to his! He wanted me to be his chauffer when his car broke down, and he had the nerve to ask me to do some of his laundry! Did I neglect to mention that this was all while I was just in high school and still living with my parents? What was that dude on? I thought that maybe I was falling in love with him, after being with him for so long. Fortunately, I never said the words. Once again, I had to move on, mentally and physically.

That's about how I begin to feel while Mannie was sexing me. I have had it with these bullshit little boys claiming to be men, these tired so-called relationships, and Ohio period. I had spent my whole life here, have not really been anywhere else. Most of my family is here, with the exception of a few on my mom's side that were scattered around. I have never been on a real

vacation or seen much of the world. I guess you

could say I have been a little sheltered. The more I

thought about it, the more upset I became. There

was only one decision to make: I'm outta here!

Reggie

"A'ight, let's go Comp!" Grier roared.

Nobody goes by their first names in the joint. Comp, short for my last name Compton was what the guards and everybody else had been calling me for the last three years. That's how long I've been in this shit hole, and now I'm finally being released.

Grier, one of the guards, was a short man with a butterball physique and thinning blond hair. He killed me always trying to be so tough. I guess he was trying to make up for his height by making everything he said echo off the walls; his way of gaining respect, which didn't faze me one bit. I had to cough to keep myself from laughing at him, and I knew that I wasn't far from leaving him and this awful place behind.

The heavy, iron gates swung open with a loud clank. I gathered my belongings; my bible, sketches, and letters from home, and began the walk from Dorm three to the discharge building a few yards away. The sun tried to peak through the grim, gray-stained cement that had been my home. I couldn't see much, but I knew it was beautiful and warm outside.

"Keep ya' head up man," Kincaid said, as I walked past his bunk.

He rubbed his graying mane of bushy hair. He looked tired and needed a shave in the worst way. I noticed the way his brown skin sagged beneath his eyes. Thomas Kincaid, my ace in this deck full of low cards. He was in for selling drugs, just like me. To be forty years old he had seen and done enough to make you think he was one hundred!

I stopped to give my man some dap, but he cut me off and looked at me strangely.

"Don't insult me like that, Comp. Give me a hug, but don't get all mushy on me!"

He extended his arms, we embraced like a father and son would on graduation day. For the first time since I found out about my release, I was kinda sad. It was as if Kincaid could read my mind because he looked me in the eye and solemnly said, "You know we'll hook up on the outside once I make parole, right?" I nodded as I let go of the embrace.

"Let's go, Comp!" Grier said angrily. "Or would you like to stay?"

"I'm comin', I'm comin'! Damn, can't a brotha say "peace" to some of his people?" I asked.

"It doesn't take that long to say one word, smartass!"

I'm being the smartass, right? I thought to myself.

I gave a final pat to Kincaid and said a few more "peace outs" to my fellow dorm mates. Once we reached the discharge building, I handed my papers to the guard at the desk. A stamp and a signature later I was on the other side of the Kentucky State Prison walls and feeling fine!

I swear this is the last time I go to prison. I must admit, I have seen my fair share of correctional facilities. Not that I was a problem child or anything, but I had made many bad decisions over the years.

I grew up in Louisville, Kentucky, home of Mohammed Ali. I knew those streets like the back of my hand. I was a quiet, skinny boy who kept to himself and stayed out of trouble. My parents often told me how I never gave them any lip or an ounce of problems, which is why it's so ironic that at twenty-five I had been locked up over twenty times since the age of sixteen. It was always over some little petty shit, like driving without a license, or using a fake ID. That is, until three years ago.

I remember it like it was yesterday, the day I was busted.

Now I am a natural born hustler, and I had been selling drugs since I was fifteen. But it was just little nickel and dime bags of marijuana. Since then, I had moved on and moved up and was selling the real deal: heroin, crack and cocaine.

I was chillin' in the brand new condo I'd bought in downtown Louisville. Man, you would have loved my crib: Vaulted ceilings, Italian leather furniture, hardwood floors, a Jacuzzi tub with chrome accenting, and my building had valet parking, and a door attendant! I even had an original Van Gogh hanging above my fireplace. The women loved that shit and I was living quite large.

I was waiting on a couple kilos of cocaine to come in from my Detroit contact, which was late on the delivery. That really pissed me off because I had a reputation to uphold and customers who were demanding my supply.

I had received a call from one of my regulars who wanted me to meet them in an alley on the other side of town. I never did business anywhere that was close to where I laid my head. I changed out of the Phat Farm sweat suit, Timberland boots, and platinum jewelry I was wearing and into a simple pair of jeans and a sweater, along with my classic Adidas sneakers. I kept my 9MM strapped on me though, cause I was damned if I was gonna get robbed.

I had one rule: If you wanted my product, you had better be there when I came. Otherwise, I was gone and would make you damn near beg to get me to sell anything to you again. I knew there were plenty of other dealers, who would have been more than happy to take my business, but my supply was the best and people knew it!

I left my Range Rover in the garage and drove my 1983 Mercury Cougar. It wasn't flashy and matched perfectly with the clothes I was wearing. Once I got to the alley, I turned my high beams on, and then turn the lights off completely, signaling my customer of my arrival. Within thirty seconds, someone should have come flyin' over to the ride where I would hook them up with whatever they needed and then I would get my dough and bounce. The whole thing took less than a minute and I wondered why I would always bother with changing clothes and cars and shit.

After forty seconds and nobody came out, I begin to pull off. Suddenly, two police cruisers pulled up: one in the front and one in the back, blocking me in the alley. I didn't even have time to blink before a big, biscuit and gravy-eatin' mothafucka pulled the door open and demanded I get out with my hands up. Before I could respond, he was reading me my rights, handcuffing me, and throwing my narrow ass into the back of his car.

At the police station, I remained calm while they interrogated me. I knew I had one hell of an attorney and they did not find much product on me. The fact that I had a gun was no big deal to me, hell; I was in a bad neighborhood and needed it for protection. That's what I was going to tell them. That probably would have worked too, but it turned out that my Detroit contact turned state's evidence on me. Once they got to him, he wanted to save *his* ass by givin' up mine. Ain't that a bitch?!

The cops had taped conversations, pictures, and signed confessions! I lost everything: The condo, my rides, jewelry, you name it. I guess I was lucky though, the judge could have thrown the book at me. However, it was my first felony. He gave me the mandatory three-year sentence with six months of parole upon my release.

So here I am, starting over from rock bottom and had nothing to show for what I had been through. I was on my way down to Atlanta where my parents and little brother were waiting for me. I hope that I can start fresh and put all that negative shit behind me. I just had to get it together and stay out of trouble! To tell you the truth I did not have much of a choice; I barely had a pot to piss in and when I was ready to throw it out, it would be from my parent's window.

During the bus ride from Louisville to Atlanta, I thought a lot about my life and what I wanted to accomplish. I knew that once I was settled, I had to go see my parole officer and get started working in my pop's restaurant, Compton and Company where I eventually would be the manager. I also had to get some pussy from somewhere! I had been satisfying myself for three damn years; I was way over due for a woman's touch, if you know what I mean.

I rested my head on the back of the seat and took in the scenery. You could tell there was a strong breeze outside by the way the trees were blowing back and forth. The sky was a clear baby blue, and the clouds looked like you could reach out and grab them.

It had been a while since I had seen my family. They relocated to Georgia soon after I had been arrested. My Pops got this great deal on this site for his restaurant and wanted to jump on it before anyone else had the chance. They still came to visit me and wrote me letters. I knew my Mom had been disappointed, but she was still there for me.

The bus finally slowed to a stop in the bus station terminal. I got up and stretched my long legs, which were aching from long ride.

Inside, the lobby was full of people going here and there, checking their luggage, and waiting for their perspective departures. Excited screams and welcome homes echoed from the walls. A family of twenty jumped up and down and yelled at the return of their young, brown-eyed solider. An older woman, about sixty or so, dropped her "Welcome Home" sign as he picked her up in his arms and twirled her around in circles. It was like everyone around had stopped their own reunions to experience the one of that family's.

Through the crowded aisle, I spotted my little brother, Rodney waving enthusiastically from across the room.

"There he is!" He shouted, and took off from my mother's hand. He pushed his way through the thick crowd, bumping and knocking people off balance. He jumped into my arms and I swung him around.

"Damn, boy you're getting heavy", I said as I stopped twirling him around. "Here, let me get a look at cha'."

My little bro was quite handsome. He had big, dark brown eyes like mine, soft, wavy hair, and his once damn-near anorexic frame had filled out to that of an athlete in the making. My mom caught up to us and scolded my little brother.

"Boy, don't you ever run away from me like that! You almost knocked those people down! We're in public, so act like you've got some home-training."

My mom, Janine pulled her long, black hair away from her face and into a ponytail. She looked good in her pink and white DKNY pants set. Her white K-Swiss sneakers were gleamin', and as usual, her makeup was flawless. Did not look like she was forty-three years old at all; never did look a day over thirty, even in her beat up, around-the-house clothes. She grabbed me and hugged me tightly.

"Hey baby, welcome to Atlanta."

"Thanks, Mama," I said.

She held my face in her hands and looked deeply into my eyes.

"Reggie, I really want you to give Atlanta a chance, okay? There is a lot you can do here to better yourself and make sure you stay outta trouble. Trust your Mama, okay?"

"Don't worry, Ma. I don't wanna go back to prison, besides I love it here already." I turned back to my brother.

"So Rodney, what you been up to? Are you playing any sports or what?"

"I ran track last year, played soccer this summer, and I'm gonna play football this year, too." He said enthusiastically with a wide smile. My brother was going to be in junior high this year and I could not believe it. Time did not seem to fly this fast while I was locked up.

"Man, you did all of that?" I asked.

"Yeah, I wanted to send you pictures of me in my uniforms and with the awards I won, but Mom thought it would be a nice surprise for you if I waited to show you when you got home." Rodney explained.

My eyes rested on my mother with a silent "thank you". She placed her arm around me and gently rubbed my shoulder, her subtle way of saying "you're welcome". When we reached the parking lot, I stopped dead in my tracks when we came up on a sparkling, navy blue Infinity coupe. The interior was baby blue with wood grain accenting, a navigation system, and a six-disk CD changer with remote.

"What's wrong, baby? Is everything alright?" My mother asked.

"Is… this… *your*… ride, Ma?" I choked out.

Rodney started cracking up. "Yeah, this is Mama's car!"

"You like it, Reggie?" Mama asked. She walked around the car, modeling it as if I was a game show contestant and it was my prize. "It's brand new, straight off the showroom floor! It only had twelve miles on it when I pulled off the lot with it!"

I studied the car thoroughly and remembered the day I bought my Range Rover. I marched right into that dealership, got the first brotha I saw, and bought it outright. That man made quite a hefty commission off me, too. I wondered what my pops was driving if my mom was cruising around in this!

We got in and I tell you, those seats where so damn soft. I could have sunk right through them! We hit the expressway, heading towards

Stone Mountain, a suburb just outside of the city.

The six-lane Atlanta highway was full of vehicles,

but the flow of traffic was steady. My mom had on

a soft jazz CD that seemed to match perfectly with

the vibe and smoothness of the car. Rodney was

going through a CD case and handed one to my

mom, asking, "Ma, can you play this please?"

"No, no, I don't feel like hearing that rap

mess right now, Rodney!" Mom said sternly.

"Save it for when we get home."

"Yeah, I'm on chill mode back here," I

agreed.

We exited the expressway and drove into

what appeared to be a very ritzy neighborhood. All

the houses were far back off the road; most of them

were two-stories and seemed to have enough land

for about two more houses to fit. The yards were

immaculate, not a weed or wilted flower in sight.

Every car you saw was one of luxury: Mercedes,

BMW's, SUV's, and a few Lexus coupes, all

washed and waxed to perfection.

"Here we are, Reggie. Welcome to your

new home!" My mother said excitedly.

I was at a loss for words: My parents' house

was the bomb!

An iron gate with "Compton" across the

middle opened and a circular driveway led us to the

front door of a gray colored, split-level stone

empire.

My pops, Calvin was standing in the

doorway, arms folded across his chest: the king of

his castle patiently awaiting his family's return. He

had not changed a bit; his clean-shaven head was

gleaming like Mr. Clean, goatee shaped perfectly,

and his stocky, six foot six frame was stylishly dressed in a cream Armani dress shirt and slacks. On his feet, cream Stacy Adams! My pops was the shit, period!

Just as I thought: I looked over towards the garage and saw that he was pushing a jet black Cadillac Escalade with twenty-two inch chrome rims and a license plate that read, "FUPAYME".

"Hey son, hiya feelin'?" Pops voice boomed.

"I'm cool, Pops. I'm just glad to be out and here with you guys." We hugged tightly.

"Well, come on, let's get you inside and settled already. You're cousins sent your things down from Louisville and they're in your room," Pops said. He gently kissed my Mom on the lips, tossed Rodney's hair, and ushered us all into the house.

Damn, it was even better on the inside!

The front hallway was a bluish-gray marble color and led to a huge oval opening. To the left was a formal dining room, complete with China place settings and Crystal wine goblets. Behind that was the kitchen, which looked like it was the set of a Food Network cooking show. Everything was black granite and chromed out! To the right was the living room, but of course no "living" was done in it. The whole room was white, even the carpeting! I would be scared to go in there with anything but my drawls on! The area behind that sprawled around and connected an informal eating area with the kitchen. Off that was the family room, where everyone chilled at, and even it was spotless!

I followed my parents up the slanted staircase that led to the bedrooms. Mine was the last one on the left. The room was huge! I had a twenty-seven inch flat screen TV, a laptop and printer, and a king size bed with satin sheets and everything. I even had my own bathroom and clothes filled the walk-in closet.

"I hope you don't mind, son," Pops interjected. "But your mother and I got a few things for you to go with what you already had. You needed some more business-like attire. You can't manage my restaurant looking like a thug, not that you ever do."

My mom tugged at my dad's arm. "Come on, Calvin. Let us let Reggie relax; it has been a long day for him. Honey, you get squared away,

then we can take you to see the restaurant and have
some dinner, okay."

"Sure Mama, I won't be too long."

"Take all the time you need, son," Pops said.
"We'll be downstairs."

My family left me to continue wandering
around in amazement. I saw my dad's office, the
master bedroom, the Jacuzzi and pool, which had a
waterfall and a slide, and the basement; a true sports
fan's haven. There were pictures of sports legends,
arenas, and teams all over the walls. A sixty-two
inch flat screen lay in the center of the back wall
and there were three huge black, suede sectionals in
front of it.

I was blown away!

After my tour, I took a long shower and
relaxed on my new bed. *Oh hell yeah, I could get*

used to this, I thought to myself. That prison shit

was for the birds and it was time once again to

move on and move up!

Karena

"Karena, you can't be serious?" Yaniya exclaimed.

I was sitting on the flowered couch in Yaniya's two-bedroom apartment. Her mini blinds were open, giving us a great view of the courtyard in her complex and brought in a ton of light to the cream-colored living room.

We had been best friends since either of us knew what a best friend was. I loved my girl to death and she was my only real friend. Niya, which I affectionately called her, was very pretty; she had long, brown hair that she always kept in a wrap style, long eyelashes, creamy cocoa skin, and a thick-in-all-the-right-places figure that dudes went crazy for.

Yaniya tapped her short, French manicured hands on the arm of the couch, awaiting my reply. You see, I had decided that I wanted to move to Atlanta; I had a cousin down there who said I could come and stay with her and her family while I got on my feet. Since I was doing absolutely nothing here in Ohio, I figured I might as well go. Yaniya and I had known each other since the first grade and had never been separated, so I knew she was gonna act all funky when I told her my plans.

"Niya, now don't start!" I scolded. "I'm working a ridiculous job; I have no man, no kids, and nothing to tie me down. Why should I stay?"

Yaniya got up from the couch with her arms folded and began pacing the room back and forth. She always did this when she was about to start whining. I thought *I* was a brat!

"K, I just don't see the point," she said in a child-like voice. "I mean, if you just have to leave, why don't you move somewhere closer like Cleveland or Cincinnati?"

I gave Yaniya a have-you-lost-your-damn-mind look and said, "Niya, kill that brat shit, alright? My mind is made up, I am closing the curtains, and soon Elvisa will be leaving the building! Besides, I thought *I* was the brat in this friendship?"

"I'm not being a brat right now and you can just…" She stopped suddenly. "Did you just say Elvisa?"

We looked at each other and started howling.

"Look," Yaniya said between chuckles, "all I'm saying is that Georgia is pretty far away.

Besides, your decision to leave is so…so…sudden. Have you really thought this all out?"

"Yes Mother, I've thought about it," I said sarcastically. "I really have and I know I'm making the right choice. If you are worried about us, our friendship, don't be. You know you're my girl!"

As much as I loved Niya, I wasn't about to ask her to come along with me! She's independent, but she is also no stranger to being a bug-a-boo sometimes. Niya was content with being a third wheel at the most inopportune times, if you catch my drift. Then she would have the nerve to get an attitude when she was asked to get lost!

If she came to kick it at my house, she was stuck up under me like it was her first time visiting and we were in elementary school all over again. I hope she understood and prayed she wouldn't dare ask me if I wanted her to come too. I would have to tell her how I felt, knowing that she would most likely take what I'd say the wrong way. This is something I wanted to do on my own, and regardless of how much I was going to miss her and my family, I just had to see what else was out there.

"So, have you told your parents yet?" Niya asked.

I stood up, grabbed my keys, and gave my friend a hug.

"I'm on my way over there now."

My father, Joel was running around the house looking for something. He took his baseball cap off and scratched his head, which was desperately in need of an appointment at the nearest barbershop!

"Lynn, have you seen those papers?" He asked.

My mother, Lynn looked away from the television. "What papers are you talking about?"

"You know the ones with the addresses of today's customers. We got four carpets to do today and I can't find those dayum papers nowhere!" He said angrily.

It was like any other Saturday morning at the Murphy residence: My dad was disorganized and running around like a chicken with its head cut off, and my mom, sister, and I were watching a decorating show on HGTV, wishing he wouldn't bother us.

I loved coming over and spending time at my former home, the place where I grew up. Right before I moved out, my dad's carpet cleaning business, Murphy and Son really picked up and the house got a much-needed makeover.

My old room had been transformed into a library-style loft with a computer and printer for my nephews when they had homework to do or wanted to surf the net. The living and dining room walls use to have this horrible wood-like paneling over them, we hardly ever had matching pieces of furniture, and our curtains were just barely hanging on. Of course, the carpets were always clean. Now, the house had beautifully buffed hardwood floors, blinds with shears around them, oriental rugs throughout, and all the furniture pieces matched perfectly and were of the finest quality.

The living room was dark brown and beige and went great with the eggshell colored walls. I was sitting in my favorite spot; the overstuffed chair in the corner of the room next to the window. In my opinion, it was the best room in the house; you could see who was coming and going outside and you had a view of the entire space, including the loft.

I was trying to hear David Bromstad's reveal of a married couple's family room on "Color Splash", but my dad was killing my concentration.

"Lynn, could you help me for a second?" He asked. "Try looking in these drawers over here. I'm gonna go look in my office." He disappeared into his office, a small room off the kitchen.

My mother sucked her teeth and jumped up from the brown, suede couch. She opened my dad's briefcase that was lying on the kitchen counter. She sighed and pulled out a few pieces of paper that were stapled together.

"Joel," she called out, "your papers were right here in your daggone briefcase!"

She closed the case, slammed the papers on top, and rejoined my sister and me in the living room just as the show was coming back from a commercial break. My dad flew into the kitchen, grabbed his things, and whizzed out of the house, mumbling something about returning later that evening.

"What's the point in Daddy even having a briefcase?" My sister, Amari asked while biting into her cream cheese-topped bagel.

Amari was older than my brother, Tony and me; she was thirty-four but didn't look older than her mid-twenties. She was a shorty; five feet zero inches just like our mom. Her jet, black hair was short, like Toni Braxton's when she first hit the music scene. Her dark skin was flawless, teeth were sparkly white, and she had a smile that lit up the room!

Did I mention what she did for a living? She had the easiest job: She did voice-overs and jingles for TV and radio commercials, did them at a studio right here in the city! She did everything from feminine spray to announcing when the evening news was coming on. She probably did ten hours of work for a whole week and got paid out the ass!

Amari lived in a huge, Victorian-style house on the eastside of town with her three boys, Timothy, Kristian, and Grayson and it was off the hook! She wasn't too flashy, though. She loved her job and the lifestyle it provided for her and her sons, but she wasn't materialistic by any means. She drove a simple Chrysler minivan and was always casually dressed: never putting on heirs for anybody!

I had just finished telling Amari and my mom about my plans of moving to Atlanta. I tried to talk loud enough for my dad, who had been in and out of the room. I don't know how much he took in, but I think he got the gist of what I wanted to do, and even seemed okay with the idea. Of course, my mom was as supportive as always, even though her baby girl was talking about leaving the only place she had ever known and was going to be hundreds of miles away.

"I think you have a great idea, baby," My mom said as she clipped coupons, preparing for her Saturday trip to the grocery store. "If you're gonna see the world, now's the time to do it!"

"She's right," Amari chimed in. "Get the heck outta dodge before you start having kids; that way you won't look back fifteen years later and wonder about what could've been."

Amari's voice had a bit of sadness to it as she spoke. My mom must have noticed it too because she lovingly rubbed Amari's hand.

"Think of what I could've had if I'd only been a little stronger and not afraid of everything!" Amari said, shaking her head. "I could've taken care of the boys a lot better if I had of stepped up to the plate sooner. Instead, I married a little boy trapped in a man's body and let him be in charge! Karena, if you feel that this is something you should do, go for it!"

Amari had gotten married young to a no-class havin', non-working, tired, trifling fool named

Lawfton. He was good looking; he was about six-
two, two hundred twenty pounds with a low fade
and goatee. Women always threw themselves at
him, but the problem was that he threw himself
right back!

Everybody knew he cheated on my sister
left, right, and sideways. However, Amari truly
believed in her marriage vows and tried to make
things work out. I guess good looks can only get a
brotha so far: She was fed up with his ass working
shitty jobs for three to six months at a time and all
that cheating! She filed for a divorce and thank
God, it became final before she started rollin' in the
doe. He would have tried his damnedest to stay!

I tried to cheer up my sister by saying,
"Amari, don't feel like that! You've done an
excellent job! You got rid of that loser of a

husband, have a career to die for, and even your
kids have changed their little demon ways!"

She playfully threw one of the couch pillows
at me, knocking the clip I had in my hair right out
and my braids spilled all over my head.

"Dang, Amari!" I said, attempting to pull
my hair back together. "But you guys are serious;
you're okay with my decision to leave?"

"Yes, Karena we're fine," Mom said. "I'm
assuming that you've already talked to Ryan about
this, correct?"

"Yes, mom, of course I did. She is thrilled
and can't wait for me to get there." I told her.

Ryan Ramirez was my cousin in the ATL.
She had lived there her whole life and we didn't
even meet each other until I was sixteen. It was at
our last major family reunion, where everybody

who lived out of town drove and flew in for the three-day event. Ryan and I began talking and promised to keep in touch with each other after she returned home.

She was married to a Puerto Rican guy named Juan; damn he was fine as hell! They had two children, Gabrielle and Juan Jr., their own financial consulting firm together, and lived in a huge house in Lithonia, Georgia, about twenty minutes outside of Atlanta.

Ryan and Juan were jazzed when I told them I wanted to move out there and they had offered to help in any way they could. They were even going to hook me up with a job in their office!

The day I called to tell Ryan, I barely got the sentence out before she exclaimed, "Ohmygosh, cuz! We would love to have you down here! I'll send you a ticket so you can come check things out first. When can you get away?"

.I called off work with the quickness and two days later I was on a plane, Georgia bound. Juan picked me up from the airport and my jaw almost hit the floor when I was their house: It was a four bedroom, ranch-style house in which Ryan had decorated personally. She was a true fan of HGTV and she and Amari were always emailing each other about this show or that one, getting different decorating ideas.

They had the softest, teal-colored carpeting I had ever stepped my feet on. All of their furniture was overstuff, my favorite, and off-white. I wondered how they managed to keep the furniture so clean but understood when Juan noticed my questioning stare and quickly stated, "Nobody eats or drinks in here."

Ryan quickly flew out of the kitchen and hugged me so hard that I almost fell over.

"Karena, I'm so glad you're finally here! It's good to see you!" She said happily.

"How was your flight? Did Juan pick you up on time? Did anybody bother you? Was traffic bad?"

"Honey, honey, slow down. She just got here," Juan said silencing the quizmaster.

"I'm sorry; I guess I'm just so happy to see you, K." We hugged again and held hands. Juan took my suitcase down the hallway and into a back room. A minute later, he returned with the kids.

"Guys, you remember Mommy and me telling you about your cousin, Karena? She's gonna be staying with us for the weekend." Juan gently pushed the kids up to me. Juan Jr. held out his hand, the perfect little gentleman.

"It's nice to meet you, cousin Karena. My name is Juan Jr. and this is my sister, Gabby."

I gently shook their little hands and replied, "It's nice to meet you both."

They were too cute! Gabby had naturally curly brown hair that hung down her back. She was wearing a red and black plaid jumper, red shirt, white tights, and black shoes. Juan Jr. was wearing jean overalls with a gray shirt and gray boots, his hair freshly faded. He was looking too fly!

Juan had an appointment and the kids went to friends' houses, so it was just Ryan and I, hanging out, drinking cappuccinos, and having good, old-fashion girl talk. Ryan pulled her slim legs up to her chest, her Mickey Mouse footies resting comfortably on the fluffy couch.

"So K," She began. "Are you dating anyone back in Columbus?"

I sipped my French vanilla liquid dream and let the flavor roll off my tongue as I swallowed.

"Not at the moment. I have a couple of admirers, but nothing steady. Why do you ask?"

I noticed a sly grin spreading over Ryan's face. Her eyes were telling me she had something up her sleeve. She coyly sipped her drink.

"Oh, I wasn't asking for any reason in particular. I was just curious. So, what kind of guys do you like?"

I eyed her suspiciously and asked, "Why do you wanna know, Ryan? What are you up to, huh?"

"What am I up to?" She asked sweetly.
"Who says I'm up to anything? We're having girl-talk, so I'm asking some typical girl-talk questions, that's all there is to it."

She could hardly suppress her smile; she was like a little kid who knew a secret that no else but her knew.

"Cut the bullshit, Ryan and tell me! You're teeth are about to bust out of your damn mouth!"

"Okay, okay!" She placed her coffee mug down. "I want us to have dinner tonight at my friends' restaurant."

"Alright," I said, not quite understanding her mood. "Is that why you're acting so giddy, just because you want us to have dinner with your friends?"

"No, you see…remember when I told you that Juan and I were gonna help you as much as we can?"

I nodded.

"Well, I think a great way for you to get used to a new city is to meet some new people. My friends, for starters, but they have two sons and the oldest one, Reggie is about your age. He's…"

"Hold it right there, Mother Love!" I interrupted. "I know you ain't tryin' to hook me up with some guy?"

Ryan held up both hands in defense. "Now wait a minute, Karena. He's really nice!"

"Uh huh, he's probably nice and ugly, right?"

"No, not right, he's a cutie pie: Dark skin, low haircut, nice teeth, and dresses really nice. I think you'd like him and I'm sure he'll like you."

"How do you know that? No you didn't…did you…did you tell him about me or somethin'?"

Ryan causally got up and strolled down the hall. "I might've said a little sumpthin', sumpthin' about my crazy, sexy, cool cousin from Ohio."

I could have high kicked her ass the rest of the way down the hall. I did not like blind dates, not one bit! They always ended up with me and some gruesome ghoul with breath hotter than the Sahara trying to feel me up and slob me down. Yuck! I was too cool on the situation. Besides, if the guy, Reggie or whatever ended up being one of those types, I didn't know if I would be able to hide my disgust. That would most likely get under her

friends' skin and I wasn't trying to create any

drama! Dammit, dammit, dammit, why did Ryan

have to go and play matchmaker?

I followed Ryan into her bedroom where she

began looking through her large walk-in closet for a

change of clothes.

"Look, Karena, Reggie just moved here

from Kentucky a few weeks ago. He's a cutie, a

sweetie, and just as cool of a person as you are,"

Ryan stated matter-of-factly. She selected a purple

peasant blouse and black dress slacks. The shirt

would look great against her light-brown skin and

she had a pair of Prada pumps that were the same

color as her top.

"I won't lie to you, cuz," She continued.

"Reggie isn't perfect, he has his flaws. But who

doesn't, especially in this day and age? All I am asking is that you have an open mind when we go to dinner, talk to him a bit and see what he is about for yourself. Since you are moving here maybe you two could hang out, get to know the city and see some of the sites together. You don't have to marry the boy, just see what's up, okay?"

I wanted to know more about the faults he allegedly had.

"Okay, Ryan you win," I said reluctantly. "But if homeboy is an off the chain, straight up mess, I'm outta there!"

"And I'll be right behind you, now go get dressed."

Compton and Company was off the hook: Smack dab in the middle of Downtown Atlanta, the restaurant had a line out the door! The valet crew speedily whipped cars in and out of the curved lot, and door attendants graciously helped customers in and out of their rides, whether they were BMWs or Beatles.

With all the fuss outside, I was surprised to see that inside it was casually classy; everyone from business execs and co-workers to coffee-drinking college students and families of four were there getting their grub on. There were two floors: the first floor held several tables and booths, as well as a bar and TV area and the second was the main dining area and had many small rooms available for those who had parties wanting a little privacy. Off the back of the first floor were a dining area and a huge dance floor with a DJ that played everything from Barry Manilow to Brandy. It was fabulous!

When we pulled up in Ryan's fire-red Lexus sedan, I watched the people waiting outside turn green with envy as she handed her keys to the valet and two handsome door attendants escorted us up to the door. Ryan tipped them and we entered the double glass doors.

I have to admit, Ryan and I were stylin' and profilin' when we walked up in there. I had changed into a casual grey dress, with my black ankle boots and matching fedora. My braids were in a flowing ponytail that hung to the side. Ryan had her long, honey-brown hair pulled up with some Chinese hair sticks, which made the ends point out in many directions. No one could tell us a thing!

One of the hosts, a cute Latina named Carmen smiled sweetly when she saw us.

"Hola, Señora Ramírez! Como esta?" She asked as they hugged.

"Muy buen, Carmen, E tu?" My cousin's Spanish sounded extremely authentic.

"Buen, buen, gracias. Mrs. Compton has been expecting you. She and her family is seated upstairs in one of the private rooms, I'll show you to the table."

Carmen led us up the winding staircase to the second floor. We entered one of the private rooms near the back of the large space. The room was immaculate and decorated in all black and gold. I noticed all the private rooms had colored themes, just something else that amazed me about the place.

"Here you are, enjoy ladies," Carmen said as she left to return downstairs.

A petite, caramel-colored woman wearing a black and gold dress jumped up from the table and rushed over to Ryan. They hugged long and tightly, like friends who hadn't seen each other in years.

"Sorry Juan couldn't make it out tonight, guys. He had to have dinner with some clients," Ryan explained.

"That's okay. It's good to see you Ryan. You look great, as always," Janine said and turned to me. "So, you must be Karena? Well, it is nice to meet you! Ryan's been going on and on about you."

I started to shake her hand, but she pushed it away and hugged me instead, just like we were family.

"Yes," Ryan announced, "this is my cousin Karena Murphy. K, this is Janine and her husband Calvin."

We shook hands.

"It's a pleasure indeed, Karena," Calvin said with a deep voice.

I didn't notice him before because Calvin was blocking my view, but when he stepped aside, I laid my eyes upon the sexiest human form of velvet chocolate I'd ever seen in my life!

"Dayum."

Did I just say that out loud?

I must have because Ryan gently nudged my arm.

"And this is Reggie. Reggie, this is Karena."

Reggie was about 5'11 and slim with a low haircut and a gorgeous smile. As we shook hands, I swear I felt a spark. I think he felt it too; we both jumped like we had touched a hot stove or something.

"Ms. Murphy is it?" He asked in a voice just as smooth as his skin. "Welcome to Compton and Company. I hope you enjoy yourself this evening."

He flashed a mind-boggling smile. I looked into a pair of dark, brown eyes that held the longest lashes I had ever seen. He was still holding my hand as he helped me into my chair. I had to make myself stop gawking at him. I felt weak, flushed. What was happening? He was just a man, that's it, that's all.

After we were all seated, Calvin ordered a bottle of Moet and encouraged me to order whatever I wanted.

"It's Courtesy of the house," Reggie stated. He winked at his father who held his glass up to him and licked his lips. I could feel myself instantly getting wet and squirmed in my seat

"Where's Rodney this evening?" Ryan asked referring to the Compton's' other son.

"We told him this was just a night for adults, so he's over at a friend's house." Janine replied.

All during dinner Reggie and I kept sneaking peeks at each other, neither of us wanting to admit our instant attraction. The others had involved themselves in business talk while we causally chitchatted. We kept the conversation to the basics: we talked about our hometowns, our jobs, how we each liked the city so far, although I didn't have much to tell him on that subject just yet. I explained why I wanted to leave Ohio and what I planned to do once I was settled in Atlanta.

"I really love Ohio; it's my home and my family and friends are there. I just think it is time for something different. Ohio is a cool place though, have you ever been there?" I asked.

"No, never been there. But I definitely see a reason to visit," He said with a slow grin.

No he doesn't call himself flirting with me!

I blushed like a schoolchild who just had her panties shown to the whole class.

"So, do you have a man back home?" Reggie asked.

"I may have an admirer or two, but nobody special. Did you leave a young lady behind in Kentucky when you came out here?"

"I had an admirer or two, but nobody special," He mocked. His eyes were locked on mine and that sent chills down my back.

Every now and then, I noticed Ryan gazing at us. She would give me that *I told you so* look with a wink, and then continue her conversation with Janine and Calvin. Reggie and I talked more about all sorts of things from who had the hottest album out to what political parties we felt were the most honest, as if there was such a thing.

Reggie was extremely intelligent and could hold a conversation about any and everything. He was so laid back, so cool and his voice remained mellow during the whole evening, even when we laughed, which was quite a bit. I felt at ease with him and as much as I liked that, it scared me at the same time. However, by the end of the night I knew I wanted to talk to him again. It was obvious that he wanted to talk to me again as well.

"So, Ms. Karena, when do you think you'll get down here permanently?" Reggie asked.

"Hopefully I'll be here within the next couple of months," I told him.

We had finished the evening and his family was seeing Ryan and me out to the car. A valet driver slowly pulled up and complimented Ryan on her ride. She, Janine, and Calvin hugged and kissed, promised phone calls and other plans to hook up.

"It was so nice meeting you, Karena," Janine said sweetly. "You make sure you get yourself back down here once you get settled, okay?"

"Sure," I said while hugging her. "And thank you so much for tonight; your restaurant is absolutely wonderful!"

Reggie held my hand as he helped me into the car. He shut the door for me and leaned in the opened window.

"I really enjoyed your company tonight, Karena. Would it be all right to call you while you are still here? Maybe we can hang out or something?"

Ryan pinched my arm.

"That would be really cool, Reggie. I don't leave until Monday morning, so give me a call."

"I'll do that."

He slowly backed away from the car but kept his eyes on me the whole time. I could not help looking back at him; he was so gorgeous! I knew I wanted to see him again and could not wait for him to call me.

At the stop light a couple blocks away from the restaurant, Ryan bounced around in her seat and clapped her hands.

"Gurrlll, what'd I tell you! He's off the hook, huh? I told you, Karena. I knew you were gonna like him! He couldn't stop looking at you for a second, even when we were leaving!"

She was right: I did like him. He was cute, cool, and he made me laugh. But I didn't want to give Ryan the satisfaction of being right, so I nonchalantly replied, "He was a'ight, seemed like a pretty smart dude."

"Oh, he was just *a'ight*, huh? So is that why you were staring at him just as hard? Is that why your jaw damn near fell through the floor when you saw him?"

Damn, the jig was up! She busted me out!

"Okay Ryan, you were right!" I said, giving in. "Reggie really surprised me. He is definitely someone I could get to know. But don't get your hopes up; I'm not looking for love."

"I know, I know, Karena. Maybe he's not either. But even when you're not looking, love will find you. Always expect the unexpected, cousin."

We rode the rest of the way in silence.

I thought about her last statement: was it possible that after all the guys I had pushed away in the past, Reggie would become my first love? The only guy who would ever hear those words to come from my beautiful lips? I chuckled to myself and shook the notion out of my head. *He's just a guy, just like the rest,* I told myself. We could hook up a few times, and if he was lucky, maybe I would let him sample the sweetness of my honey pot and we could do the damn thing! But that is as far as it would go. When it comes to men, love has nothing to do with it!

Reggie

"Reggie, Karena's on the phone for you!"
Rodney yelled.

I felt my heartbeat accelerate as I reached
across my bed for the phone.

"I got it, Rod!" I hollered. As I listened, I
heard him click off the downstairs phone.

"Hey baby?" I asked.

"Hey handsome, how are you?" She asked.
Damn, she had the sexiest voice!

"I'm good, really good now that I'm talkin'
to you. So, what's goin' on?"

"Well, I wanted to call and let you know that
I'll be coming into town tomorrow afternoon. I was
hoping we could see each other."

It had only been three weeks since we met
that night at dinner. I could not take my eyes off

her; she had this cool and classy way about her. We talked the whole time and she had totally mesmerized me.

She said it was cool to call her, so the next day I did. I invited her over to our house and we went downtown to The Underground; it used to be part of the Underground Railroad and now it has turned into a place that has lots of little shops, vendors and restaurants. We had a great time just laughin' and jokin' around. I helped her pick out some souvenirs for her peeps back home, and then we had lunch at Johnny Rockets, and old-fashion diner-type joint.

Afterwards, we went to the park that's around the corner from my house and talked for hours. It was beyond dark by the time she headed home and I made her promise to call me once she got there safely. I was having such a good time with her; I didn't want her to leave. She made me feel at ease, comfortable, as if we had known each other for years. I ain't even going to lie; Karena had my nose open somethin' tough! I had a serious jones for her.

After she went back to Ohio, we talked on the phone, texted every day, and emailed each other. I don't have to tell you what my phone bill was like! Her conversation and off-the-hook vibe was well worth every penny!

I knew I had to tell her about me being locked up and when I finally did, I was scared to death; I didn't know how she was going to react. I wasn't exactly sure if we would eventually develop a relationship, but I wanted her to know about my prison past before we got any closer to that

happening.

We were having one of our many three-in-the-morning phone conversations. Her voice was even sexier at night and I didn't know how to tell her, so I just came right out and said it.

"Karena, I was in prison before I came down here."

Oh yeah, Comp, that was smooth!

I didn't mean to blurt it out like that; it was just that I was so nervous. I was glad that I could not see her facial expression at that moment. She was quiet and for a second I thought that she had hung up on me, and then I heard her take a deep breath.

"So that's what you were doing up there in K Y? What happened?"

I ended up spilling the beans; I told her everything that had led up to my arrest and why I was nervous about telling her.

"Reggie, if we're going to be friends or whatever, you have to talk to me. What did you think I was going to say? 'Fuck that dude 'cause he just got out of the joint?'"

"Well..."

"Oh come on now! I know we don't know each other *that* well, but I hope you would not think that I am that judgmental. Everyone makes mistakes, honey."

At that moment, I knew there was a reason why I thought she was so easy to talk to, and I instantly regretted not telling her the truth sooner. The point was that she did not head for the hills when I did and she actually respected me more for being honest. Yep, home girl definitely had possibility.

Even though Karena was not coming back down here to stay permanently just yet, she said her sister had to come to the city to handle some business and that she was going to tag along. I could not wait to see her!

The day of Karena's arrival was the bomb: the sun was shining, the sky was the clearest form of blue I had ever seen, and the weather was perfect at a mild seventy-two degrees.

I was feeling nervous and anxious all morning; I just could not sit still. I knew I was driving my family crazy, but I think they were secretly enjoying it. I had never been this way over a female before.

I must have changed my clothes three times before I decided on a matching blue jean jacket and pants with a beige shirt and my Timberland boots.

"Reggie, how many more times are you going to change?" My mother had been watching me from the doorway of my bedroom.

"I just want to make sure I'm lookin' good, Mama," I replied.

She walked over and sat down on the bed, patting the space next to her so I could join her.

"Baby, you must really like Karena, huh?"

"Yeah, she's on point."

"Come on now, don't play that macho, I'm-with-my-boys-from-around-the-way type of game with me! I'm your Mama; I know what the deal is."

I wanted my mom to know how I was feeling about Karena, but I didn't feel right discussing the whole nine yards with her. That was a conversation for me and Pops, so I tried to tell her something that would pacify her.

"Look Ma, we just met. I don't know what will happen. Yes, I do like her. I like her a lot. She is very nice and extremely smart. We had a good time when she was here last."

Mom kissed me and got up to leave.

"Reggie, I've never seen you act this way over any other girl. I know you like her more than you're willing to say."

I left the house and went to holla at a few of my cousins. They were on my pop's side of the family and lived over in Decatur. As soon as I pulled up to the modest three-bedroom house, I saw my older cousin, Spanky sitting outside on the porch and puff, puff, puffing away on a Black and Mild cigar.

"Whatcha know good, Reg?" He asked, with smoke pouring out his mouth. We gave each other some dap with a one-arm hug.

"Man, you know I can't call it. Let me get one of those Blacks."

Spanky was a light-skinned dude with brown eyes and long dreadlocks, which he had pulled back in a ponytail. Women went nuts for this cat! He couldn't go anywhere without a female foaming at the mouth over him, and it didn't matter if they were married or involved or what.

Spanky used to take advantage of that shit; he would fuck as many women as he could, play with their minds, and spend their hard-earned money. However, one broad he fucked named

Dianna had my man burning like a forest fire in Cali! After that, he chilled the hell out. Now he only has one girl, Crystal; he is very much in love with her and they are supposed to get married next spring.

I started rolling the cigar between my hands so that the tobacco inside would spill out into the plastic wrapping. Once it was all out, I removed the filter from inside, then gently refilled the hollow shell with the tobacco, packing it down inside with a pencil to make sure I got as much as I could back in. This is called "freakin" a Black and Mild, the best way to smoke one in my opinion.

After I took a hit of the lit cigar, I let my mind wonder a bit. Spanky was on his cell phone talking to Crystal. He turned into a different person almost when he talk to or about her; his voice got all soft, he got this puppy-dog look in his eyes, hell, homeboy even started blushing sometimes! Anybody who knew him could tell how much he loved old girl. Seeing a reformed player like Spanky fall head-over-heels in love with a woman made me think there was hope for me, maybe even with Karena.

"You just missed Buster and Peanut, Reg," Spanky said after closing his cell phone.

"Damn, where they roll off to?"

"Oh, they went to go kick it with some skank-ass broads over in East Point; met them at some club, so you already know the deal."

"They still fuckin' with them club hoppin', fuck-any-nigga-for-a-ride-in-your-caddy type broads?"

"Hell yeah, and you know what? My ignorant ass woulda been right with 'em if I hadn't of met Crystal. I'm tellin' you cuz, that girl save my life!"

"Yeah, I feel you."

We continued to talk about Buster and Peanut. To be honest, I was worried about them: not because they were my family, but also because they were Y.B.Ms (young black males) and we had enough problems to confront without having to worry about fucking some broad with a disease. They were both grown-ass men though and they can handle their own shit. I had better things to do.

My cell phone rung: it was Karena.

"Hey baby, where you at?" I asked eagerly.

Karena laughed her little-girl laugh. I loved that shit!

"Were you expecting my call or somethin'?" She asked. "Anyway, we're at the airport."

"Want me to come and pick you guys up?"

"Naw babe, we're getting a rental car, but thanks for asking. Just meet me at the hotel in about an hour and a half; it's the Hilton downtown, room 618."

"Cool, I'll be there."

I hung up and Spanky was looking dead at me, smiling.

"So, it's like that huh?" He asked.

"What?"

"*What*? Reggie please! Your nose is more open than a porno star's pussy! How long is she in town for and when you bringing her through so I can meet her?"

I shook my head and headed towards my ride.

"Soon, man, soon. I gotta bounce, there's somethin' I gotta do."

Damn, this place is off the hook! I thought to myself.

I had never been to this hotel before and I quickly noticed that you had to have some serious dough to stay up in here. And to think, Karena and her sister were going to be here for a week!

There was a large, grand piano in the middle of the lobby, with plenty of leather seating around it for those who wanted to listen or just rest their feet. The dining room was dimly lit, creating a nice romantic atmosphere, and the bar was well stocked with everything from Moet to wine coolers. The whole scene looked like something out of a magazine.

I walked across the marble floors and plush carpeting towards the mirrored elevators; the buttons were gold accented. On the way up, I took a few last looks at myself, making sure everything was the way it was supposed to be.

My hands were shaking as I knocked on the door to room 618. You would think I had never seen Karena before, or that I didn't know she was going be here. I cuffed my hand over my mouth. *Does my breath smell all right? I knew I should have got some gum before I came here! What if she doesn't like my clothes?* I took a deep breath; man, I was trippin'! Suddenly, the door flew open and there she stood.

She was a vision of perfection.

"Hey handsome, I missed you!" Karena said. She pulled me into the room and hugged me tightly. I returned the embrace and did not want to let go.

"I missed you too, baby. Here, these are for you."

I handed her the coral-colored, long-stem roses I had bought on the way over. Karena's face lit up.

"Reggie, these are beautiful!" She exclaimed.

"I thought I could get you a little something. Step back, let me look at you."

She backed away from me and spun around, striking poses here and there. She was wearing a pink cardigan sweater over a black shirt, black jeans, and black boots. Here braids hung down past her shoulders.

"You like it?" She asked.

I licked my lips, silently showing her how much. I wanted to rip those clothes right off her body and throw her down onto one of the queen-sized beds. I was hoping to kiss her today or at least some time while she was here, seeing how it would not have been too appropriate to do so the last time we were together.

Karena grabbed my hand and pulled me inside. She filled an empty bottle with water and placed the roses inside, then led me to the bed; she took her boots off and sat down with her feet up. I sat at her feet towards the middle of the bed and tickled her.

"No, please Reggie, don't tickle me!" She was crackin' up!

"I didn't know you were that ticklish. I'll try not to do that anymore, but it's gonna be hard!"

She ushered for me to sit next to her at the top of the bed. I kicked my boots off and climbed up next to her. When I sat down, Karena started rubbing the top of my head slowly. Damn, that felt good.

"Your hair is so soft, I like the way it feels."

"I like the way *you* feel when you do that"

I looked into her eyes; she was focused on me and her eyes told me that she was feeling the same way I was: horny as hell! I hadn't gotten any since I had been out. I mean, I got my dick sucked a few times by some freak my cousin introduced me to, but I was not about to fuck her; she was only good for that one thing. I had wanted Karena since the first time we met; she was so sexy and I absolutely love the full figured women, damn those skinny-ass broads!

Karena's perfume had me in an intoxicating daze. I was nervous at first and could tell she was too, but we both knew what we wanted. I decided to go for it and softly kissed her sexy, full lips. Damn, not only were her lips as smooth as silk, they also tasted oh so sweet!

I had to fight the urge to deep-tongue her, that is until she got me first. I felt her tongue on mine and together they did a wet version of a doe-see-doe.

I held her face in my hands, caressing her skin gently. Karena explored my body with her hands, starting at the nape of my neck. I was as hard as a brick! She unbuttoned my shirt and began rubbing my nipples. *Oh shit, that's my spot!* All the while, we were still kissing; my hands were all over her! Suddenly, Karena stopped and looked into my eyes, we were both breathing hard.

"My sister is gonna be gone for a while, at least until nine or ten tonight."

She had a longing in her voice, a desire that whispered her want for my touch. I knew there was no turning back now.

We continued our tongue dance with more passion than before. I took my jacket and shirt off, my muscular chest and abs exposed, showing Karena that I regularly worked out. Her fingers felt so good running across my body.

I found my way under her shirt, unsnapped her front-hook black lace bra and swirled my tongue around her nipples. Karena started to moan; she rubbed the back of my head and grabbed my shoulders in appreciation.

I fumbled around with her belt buckle, eventually unbuttoning her pants. I slowly pulled them down and tossed them to the side. I unzipped my jeans with the quickness and threw them next to hers. Karena continued to nibble and lick her way all over my body. When she got to my bottom half, she began to stroke my manhood through my silk boxers. She bent down and slowly started trying to hide it in her mouth. I swear my whole dick damn near disappeared!

"Ohhhhhh, shit!" I moaned.

I was on cloud ninety-nine; the girl had some serious skills!

She bobbed and weaved her head up and down; her rhythm was as smooth as the horses on a Merry-Go-Round. It was as if I was a giant drink and Karena was thirsty as hell; she slurped and sucked my shit like she was trying to get the last drop. She moaned as if she was the one getting pleased and the vibration of her mouth made me want to scream like a little bitch! She stopped and teased the head of my dick, quickly flicking her tongue back and forth.

"Gatdamn! Oh shit, that's it!"

I thought I was about to bust and I didn't want to cum yet; I wanted to be inside her. I was ready to submerge myself in her.

"Your turn, baby"

Now I had been with many women and have had sex more times than I could count, but never had I ever experienced sex with a woman who got as wet as Karena did! I mean, it was as if she was dripping through her damn panties! I could have cum right then and there, but I managed to compose myself and slid her panties off. Her pussy was throbbing, pulsating like a heartbeat. I held on to the back of her thighs and plunged my tongue deeply inside her.

"Ahhh!" Karena moaned in ecstasy.

She tasted like chocolate and strawberries and I lapped up as much of her juices as possible. I gently bit her clit and she cried out, not because I had hurt her, but because it felt so damn good. She shoved my head farther down and held it there as if she was daring me to move it. The more she pushed the deeper and faster I went, sending Karena into orgasmic spasms. Her body jumped and jerked all over that damn bed like she was being electrocuted.

"Ahhh baby I'm about to cum!"

I eased my head up from her wetness.

"No baby, don't stop," She begged, but I had more work to do.

I kissed her up and down her legs then on the lips, tonguing her so that she could sample her own juices.

I grabbed a condom and could barely get it on; my hands were shaking with anticipation. Once I made sure it was on nice and tight, I looked Karena dead in her eyes; I wanted to make sure she knew what was about to go down.

Lord, please don't let me bust a nut too quickly!

I entered her and she welcomed me warmly. We created a perfect fit, her body and mine. I tried to go slow, tease her a bit. But her warmth and wetness made it impossible, and I began quick thrusts.

"Go deeper Reggie, deeper," She moaned.

I hoisted Karena's legs up and plunged in. If I could have gotten into her any deeper, all you would have seen would have been my toes dangling out!

Karena screamed out and raked her nails across my back.

"Yes, baby! Oh Reggie, that's it baby!"

I felt myself getting close to climaxing, but I was not done with her yet. I pulled myself out.

"Lemme hit it from the back."

"That's my favorite position, baby. Make sure you smack my ass, too."

So she likes that freaky shit, huh?

I entered her and commenced to smackin' her ass like she was a demon possessed heathen! I grabbed a handful of Karena's braids and pulled, her moans increased an octave as her back arched. I placed my hands on her waist and started bucking. I bucked through all the frustration I had felt while being locked up. Bucked for the three years I had spent deprived of having sex. With every stroke her pussy curved to my dick, tightly and unyielding. I bucked, and bucked, and bucked us both into a spine-tinglin', toe-curlin', body-jerkin' orgasm.

"Oh Reggie, I'm cummin'! I'm cummin', baby! Don't stop!"

"Karena! Oh shit, this pussy is soooo good!"

We both collapsed, sexually exhausted and dripping with sweat. I rolled off her and onto my back; Karena laid her head on my chest.

"Baby, that was amazing!" I said breathing heavily.

"It sure was; I've never cum that hard before!"

Karena kissed me softly; her lips were salty from our mixed natural juices. Holding her in my arms made me realize how much I like the feeling; how I wished I could go to sleep with her every night and wake up to her every morning. I know I wasn't whipped, not sexually anyway. The sex being so damn good was just the icing on the cake. Karena had my mind; she stimulated me mentally in more ways than I ever thought possible and I knew she had won my heart.

"Karena, let's get married!"

What the hell did I just say?

"What did you just say?! Karena exclaimed, as if she had read my mind. She immediately sat up and pulled the sheets up over her exposed breasts.

I had surprised myself; there I went blurting shit out again! I was thinking in my mind how it would be if we were to get married, but I didn't mean to say the shit out loud!

Karena stared at me as if I was losing my damn mind. However, you know what's funny? The more confused she appeared to be, the more certain I was of the statement I had just made. She was the one, period. I had "wifed her up" that night at the restaurant, you know, imagined what she would be like if she ever became my wife. That image had not left my mind since then, and in fact, it had only gotten clearer as the weeks passed.

"Reggie, I know you didn't say what I think you just said."

I took her hand in mine and looked directly at her.

"Yes, you heard me right, and I'm dead serious."

Karena breathed deeply and tousled her already wild braided mane.

"Reggie, I know the sex was good, but…"

"This has nothing to do with sex."

She raised an eyebrow.

"Well, it has a little to do with that. But the bottom line is that I realized that I wanna be with you, and I know you wanna be with me too. I'm not suggesting that we do it right away, I just wanted you to know that you're the one I wanna marry."

The room was silent and all you could hear was our deep breathing. *What if she shoots me down? What if she laughs in my face?* Man, I would feel like the biggest idiot in the world!

"Okay."

My thoughts were interrupted.

"I'm sorry, what did you say Karena?"

"I said 'okay'. We can get married."

I eyed her suspiciously; she noticed it.

"I'm serious. If you want to get married and you're really sure about it, then okay."

I kissed Karena hard and long. I had so many plans for my future; plans that did not include another stay at Château de Prison, and I wanted Karena Denise Murphy to be a part of them. I had the bomb job and now the bomb woman!

Everything was everything.

Karena

"Niya, girl I'm on my way! I know I'm runnin' a little late, but I'm stuck on the freeway; 70 westbound is backed the hell up clear past Livingston Avenue! I'll get there as soon as I can."

I absolutely, without a doubt hated traffic! Interstate 70 was jammed and I was smack dab in the middle of it, bumper to bumper. People were hollering out of their windows speaking every curse word known to man and laying on their horns. Unfortunately, I was also one of the ones participating in that childish behavior, but hey, I told you I hated traffic.

It had been a week since Amari and I returned from our Atlanta excursion and I was finally able to kick it with my girl, Niya. It was crazy when we got home; I had a ton of unpacking to do, and I had to go back to work the next day!

I had spent most of the week going in to work early and staying after work late, trying to make up some of my missed hours. When I got home, I talked to Reggie and then I would pass out in my bed for the night. Niya had been calling me all week at home, work and on my cell. I tried to tell her what the deal was, but she was not trying to hear it.

"So, are you frontin' on me now, K?"

"Yaniya, what the hell are you talkin' 'bout?"

"You know what the hell I'm talkin' 'bout! You spent a week in Atlanta, probably all stuck up under that dude. You've been back for a week, and you haven't called or came by yet!"

You know, sometimes I felt as if I was Yaniya's only friend!

"Look, my bad girl, but I told you what was up! I'll tell you what: I won't work late tomorrow and we can hook up, go to happy hour or something. What do you say?"

"Alright, tomorrow then, but don't play me Karena!"

Shit, I should have known there was gonna be all this traffic, and it's Friday and a payday, too!

Fuck this!

As soon as I could, I darted over to my far right lane and exited onto Keller Avenue. I took the streets the rest of the way from the eastside to Easton, one of our entertainment spots in the city. Niya and I were meeting up at this restaurant and bar called Ocean's. It had been one helluva long day and I really needed a drink.

To be honest, I was really in no mood to hang out with Niya, but I felt like I owed it to her for not being around all week. I don't know what was going on with me lately, but I was losing my desire to be with my best friend. Was that normal? It couldn't have been; we had been best friends forever. Now, it was like we were growing apart or more as if I was the one who was growing apart from our friendship.

I found a great parking spot right outside the door to Ocean's, which was damn near impossible to do on a Friday night. I reluctantly entered and made my way upstairs to the second level where the bar was and where Niya wanted me to meet her.

I had to take a few deep breaths, hoping to remove the bad feelings I had about the pending evening and managed to put on a smile when I saw my girl waving me over from across the room. Niya looked great in her brown leather jacket and skirt ensemble. Her hair was freshly crimped and shiny.

"Girl, I thought you would never get here!" She said.

We sat down at the oval marble table and Niya sipped her Sex on the Beach.

"Sorry, I came straight from work, but traffic was a bitch, as usual."

"It's cool; I already ordered a drink for you."

"Thanks. So what's been up?"

"Well, Ty and I went out; he took me to Eddie Merlot's!"

Eddie Merlot's was a hot new restaurant on the North side of town. It was supposed to be very nice. It was also expensive, but most of the people I talked to said the prices were worth it; the food was amazing.

Ty Benson was Yaniya's latest victim; he was a honey brown-skinned college boy with beautiful hazel eyes and curly hair. His family was allegedly rich, something Niya had heard through the gossip grind, but he seemed to be just another average Joe, straight out of an Old Navy ad.

Ty was mad cool, which is why I felt bad for him hooking up with Niya. Now don't get me wrong; I am not hater! I want Niya to get hers, but she was just playing that boy! She wanted to see if in fact, there was a family fortune and how much of it he was willing to spend on her.

Niya wasn't a true gold digger, but she did have the traits. It was no secret that she wanted to live the high life and unfortunately, her job did not provide the means for that to occur. Therefore, whenever she got with a guy who even looked like he had a smidge of funds, she was all over him!

My drink arrived and I took a sip. I ordered the chicken fingers basket with fries and Niya wanted the loaded nachos. While we awaited our food, I barely got a word in; I was too busy being briefed on my friend's latest dramatic episode.

"That restaurant was off the hook, K! And I don't even wanna tell you how much money Ty spent on dinner!"

Yeah, but I am sure you will!

As if she was reading my mind, she blurted out, "One hundred and twenty-five dollars and girl I didn't have to pay for shit!"

"So, you finally one with some money," I said, trying to sound interested.

"Well, you know how it is."

I rolled my eyes and hoped she didn't notice.

Finally, our food came and we dug in. I was too consumed by my growling stomach and my throbbing coochie to pay attention to Niya. I missed Reggie. She snapped her fingers in my face.

"Karena, damn, can you hear or what?"

"I'm sorry, what did you say?"

"I was asking you about your trip. Did you see your boy? Did you finally let him hit it or what?"

I could no longer hide my irritation.

"Yaniya, that's none of your damn business!"

Her face dropped to the floor and into a million pieces. She looked genuinely hurt by my response.

"Why you bitin' my damn head off? And since when haven't we been in *each other's* business? We tell each other everything!"

"I'm sorry; I didn't mean it to come out like that. The trip was great; I spent a lot of time with Reggie, and yes, we did get down. That shit was good, too!"

That perked her back up! Yaniya was a big freak and anything about sex, minus that sadomasochist shit, turned her on. She probably touched herself thinking about some of the sexual encounters I had shared with her. I never told her all the details, just enough to get her to quit badgering me about them. However, I was being extra tight-lipped about Reggie. What we shared was not just sex, it was deeper than that, and I wanted to keep it to myself.

"Well?" Yaniya was almost foaming at the mouth to get some answers out of me.

"Well what?"

"Oh come on Karena? Exactly how good was it? Tell me what the brotha was workin' with!"

"Like I said, the shit was good and that's all you need to know."

"Okay, I get it now; homeboy was weak but you kinda feelin' him, so you don't wanna hurt his feelings by admitting it. I see you."

"No Ms. Final Analysis, you don't see me. Reggie was far from weak, it's just that…well…you just don't need to know all the details, Niya."

I could tell her pride was injured, but I was standing my ground on this. Yes, it was true that Niya and I always talked about things and she knew about most of my sexual experiences, just as I knew about hers. But I'm a firm believer in the fact that some things are better left unsaid. It's not like I didn't trust her, it's just that knowing every detail about every sexual encounter I had ever had was simply unnecessary, even for my best friend.

"I don't believe you! Why are you holdin' out on me, K?"

I sucked my teeth; I was getting really irritated with this conversation!

"I'm not holding out on you, it's just that, never mind. Let's change the subject: I'll tell you something that'll make your eyes bug outta your head."

"I'm listening."

"Reggie asked me to marry him and I said yes."

Niya spewed her drink out all over the table. I swear, I thought my girl was about to hit the floor!

"He did what?! You told him what?!"

"You heard me."

"Karena, have you lost your damn mind? Marry him? Ya'll have only known each other for a fuckin' month!"

The couple at the next table looked over at us, wondering what was going on. I shot them a stay-the-fuck-over-there-and-mind-yours look.

"For your information, it's been six weeks and Yaniya lower your voice! Look, Reggie can't be serious, alright? We had just finished having sex and had barely caught our breath when he suggested that we get married. It was probably just his dick talking."

"If you know he's not serious, than why did you say yes?"

"I said yes because I didn't want to leave him there lookin' like Booboo the Fool. I figured I'd play along. Girl please, I am far from the marriage scene. Besides, it's going to take a long time before Reggie could get me to go there, if he could at all."

"Well, it sure didn't take him long to have you crawlin' outta your panties!"

I threw a French fry at her.

Niya and I spent over two hours up in that place! After our bellies were full and we were feeling nice from our drinks, we left Ocean's and walked around the outside part of the mall. It was very cool out and the wind was whipping our hair all around. Niya was going off because she had just been to the salon.

"Fuck this; I just got my wig busted! If we keep walkin' around out here I won't have crimps anymore; the wind will blow them all out!"

I was alright with us being outside: ah, the joy of having braids! Rather than listen to her bitch and moan I figured it was best if we just went ahead inside. We went to the second floor, copped a couple of seats in front of Smokin' Joe's Café and looked down at the many people going here and there. The line for movie tickets were just below us and it was long as hell! Even the line for the pay by credit card machine was long. I'm glad she wasn't trying to go see a movie; I didn't want to put up with all those people!

I was beyond ready to go home, so I told Niya I would holla at her later and left. I had forgot to put my cell on vibrate once I got in the bar, so I had missed Reggie's call. I got in the car, programmed my MP3 to play Maxwell's "Now" C D, and checked my messages on my way home.

"Hey baby, it's Reggie. I just wanted to call and hear ya voice. I miss you. I miss bein' inside you, miss makin' you cum."

My panties were wet. The mere sound of his voice made my panties wet.

"I wish you didn't have to leave, but we both have something to look forward to when you get

down here for good. Anyway, I'm busy tonight and the restaurant is stacked! If you call, I'll do whatever I have to do to make sure we can talk, even if it's for a minute. So hit me back when you can. Oh, by the way, I love you Karena. Peace."

I almost swerved off the road! Did he say he loved me? Reggie and I had to have a serious talk!

I was lying on my bed replaying Reggie's message for the umpteenth time. I made sure the TV and radio were off, and that there was no background noise. I just had to make sure that I heard his message loud and clear. I did; he said he loved me! My heart skipped a beat. I was happy! I couldn't believe it, I was genuinely happy about Reggie loving me.

I thought about the time we had spent together on my last visit; it was like we belonged with each other, just like Reggie said. We had a wonderful time: we went on the CNN studio tour, to the Atlanta Contemporary Arts Center, and got lost too many times to count while we zigzagged through the city. Not to mention that he had my back and legs aching from all the sex he put on me! That man had me twistin' and turnin' all over that bed, and had me screaming obscenities that would've made Hugh Hefner blush! He really held it down in between the sheets, outta the sheets, on top of the sheets...

Well anyway, I had introduced Reggie to my sister that Sunday we were in town. We went over to Compton and Company and had lunch then went over to the Lennox Mall for some shopping. Reggie didn't complain one bit and enjoyed the little fashion show we put on for him while we were trying on one outfit after another. Amari took to him really well, and by the end of the day, it was like they had known each other for years.

"He seems like a really nice guy Karena, and very mannerly," Amari said.

We had just returned to the hotel and I was beat! Reggie and I had early plans for the next morning: he wanted me to go with him while he went apartment hunting and I wanted to get some sleep.

Amari had changed from her navy blue sweats and sneakers and into her leopard print nightgown. She sat down at the desk and whipped her laptop open; she had a meeting first thing in the morning. I wrapped my braids up in my black silk scarf, threw on my raggedy gray sleep shirt, and climbed into the bed.

"It's obvious that you two really like each other," She said, never looking up from the fifteen-inch screen. "So, are you guys gonna hook up when you move here?"

"Hook up?"

"Yeah, you know, make things official?"

"Amari hold up, we just met. I mean, of course we'll probably hook up to go to the movies and do stuff like we did today. But if you mean "hook up" as in "start a relationship" I doubt it."

"Why do you make it sound like that idea is so far-fetched?"

"It's not that, but I mean...Have you seen all the men that are running around down here? We've only seen bits and pieces of the city, so I can only imagine! I could barely keep my eyes focused on Reggie without looking at every other dude that passed our way. I'm just sayin'; I don't think I

should hire Reggie permanently if I know I still

wanna interview other applicants."

Amari looked up from her computer; she

was giving me that "yeah right" face.

"Okay, whatever you say, Karena. But I

know you like that boy."

"I never said I didn't, but I'm not looking to

get into a relationship right now, that's all."

Amari shrugged her shoulders and turned

her attention back to her laptop. I propped up my

set of pillows and tried to fall asleep, but I had a

hard time because my mind kept drifting to Reggie.

After every time I'd finish being with him or talking

to him it took me forever to come down off the high

he gave me.

I never was the kind of woman who believed in fronting, so I didn't do it very often. Admitting I had feelings for Reggie was weird for me. I just didn't want to be played, or fall in love with some man who would only end up breaking my heart. That Reggie; he must have put some kind of spell on me or something!

I tried not to think about Reggie every minute of the day, but it was impossible. When I wasn't talking to him, I was thinking about talking to him. When we were talking, I was thinking about being with him. No other guy had ever made me feel the way he did, or treated me as well. Reggie's manners were unreal; he was chivalrous and always wanted to know what I was thinking or feeling.

Maybe he was just running game. That was possible, seeing how he had just gotten out of prison. Maybe he just wanted me because I was the first girl he'd been with once he got out. I didn't think that was the case: something about his words and the way he said them told me he was being honest.

My phone rang, jarring me from my thoughts.

The caller I D was flashing: *Georgia Call.*

"Hello?"

"Hey, baby!"

"Reggie, hey I was just about to call you."

"Sure, tell me anything. So how was your day?"

"It was long and tiring. I would ask how yours is going but it's not over yet."

"Naw, not by a long shot, but it's going well. Did you get my message?"

"Yes, as a matter of fact I did. I wanted to talk to you about that."

"Which part did you wanna discuss; the part where I said that I missed makin' you cum, or the part where I said I love you?"

"The last part, that's the one."

"Are you okay that I told you that? I mean, I wanted to say it to your face when you were here, but I couldn't get up the nerve. I know, I know I punk'd out. But I needed to tell you."

"No baby, it's not that I have a problem with you saying that. I always want you to be honest with me about what you're feeling, no matter what it is. It's just that…that…"

"It's just that what? Karena, what's wrong?"

I nervously twirled one of my braids around my index finger. I had been prepared to let him down; tell him that I thought he was cool people, but that I didn't want to be with him like that. I had been prepared to move down to Atlanta and "sow my royal oats" if you will, by dating other eligible bachelors. Never in a million years had I been prepared to fall in love, and I did. It just hit me: I was head over heels in love with Reggie!

"Karena, are you still there?"

"Oh yeah, sorry baby, I'm still here. I guess I just had a brain fart or something."

"You had a what?! Look, is everything alright?"

"Yes Reggie, everything's fine. I just wanted to tell you that I loved your message; and I love you too."

Reggie breathed what I think was a sigh of relief.

"You really love me?" He said quietly.

"Yes, I really do."

"Karena, I don't think you realize how happy you just made me. Look, check this out: I gotta get back to work. But I'm gonna try and call you when I get off so that I can hear your voice before I go to sleep, a'ight?"

"A'ight, have a good night."

"You too."

I had to make myself hang up. It was like the phone had melted onto my ear and I was in this hypnotic state. I was in love, for the first time ever! As hard as it was to admit that to myself the words just happened to fall easily from my lips. Ryan had been right: love had found me and I found it in

Reggie. I knew there was no turning back now and

so it began!

Yaniya

Damn, that Karena was somethin' else!

I was right in the middle of getting some of

the best head I've ever gotten in my life when she

called. At first I had let the call roll over to my

voice mail, because what girl do you know will

have a man stop eating her out just so she can jump

up and answer the damn phone? The phone just

continued to ring and I knew only one person would

keep calling me like that.

"Oh no, now is not the time for this

bullshit!" I moaned. Ty was workin' every one of

his tongue muscles and I was so close to climaxing!

This was the wrong time for fuckin' phone calls!

"Hold up baby, I'll bet that's Karena, so

lemme see what she wants. But keep your head

right where it is!"

I grabbed the phone in a huff.

"Hellooo?" I breathed in my sexy nighttime voice.

"Niya, what's goin' down girl?"

Damn the sexiness in my voice because now I was frustrated!

"It's not *what's* goin' down, it's *who's* goin' down and that person is Ty! He was right in the middle of eatin' my pussy and doin' a mighty fine job of it too before you called. So what's good? Why you sound like that?"

Karena started giggling like a schoolgirl, which pissed me off even more. Ty lifted his head and wiped my nectar from his mouth. I rolled my eyes at him.

"Girl, you'll never guess what just happened!" Karena said gleefully.

"Karena, I was right in the middle of something and I'm in no mood for guessing games, so just spit it out so I can continue to get mine."

"Okay, okay. I told Reggie I loved him."

"Big deal, you also said you would marry him and we both know you weren't serious!"

"Well maybe not about the marriage thing but I am serious about loving him. See he left me a message while we were out saying how much he missed me and stuff. At the end of it, he said he loved me! Of course, I was thinking he was just trippin', but when he called the crib later on and we talked, I realized that I was in love with him so I told him. You should've heard the happiness in his voice!"

"So just like that: you're in love with him? Not even five hours ago, he was just someone to kick it with in the ATL. Hell, five hours ago you were so-called "still interviewing". Now you're in love? Duh, okay Karena, whatever you say!"

"For real, I'm serious! Why are you hatin'?"

Now I was a hater? I had to give her the professional-anchor-on-the-six o'clock-news voice.

"Well, this concludes our evening broadcast. Tune in tomorrow!"

I hung up the phone. Karena was always the one hating on me about the clothes I wore and the men I dated. She was probably secretly mad right now because Ty was over here handling his business and the man she allegedly "loved" was all the way the fuck in Georgia and couldn't handle her cooch right now!

I thought she was hurt or something and all she wanted to say was that she was in love? I stopped my man from continuing his hearty meal to answer her call and she had the nerve to say *I* was a hater! That shit really burned me up!

Ty was sitting at my feet lookin' like a wounded bird. I was ready for him to get back down there for seconds, so I tried to butter him up.

"Ty, what's the matter boo?"

"Did you have to let the world know I was over here eatin' your pussy?"

Holy shit, was he for real?

"That was not the world on the phone, it was Karena. She had something very important to tell me."

"Yes I heard. But did she need to know what I was doin'?"

I tried to maintain my composure and stifle the attitude I felt coming on. I crawled down to Ty and began placing soft kisses all over his hairy chest. His abs was so defined it looked like someone had drawn them on!

"Boo," I said sweetly, "it was only Karena. She's my best friend so what's the big deal? Do you think she doesn't already know that we're having sex and good sex at that?"

"You talk in detail about our sex life?"

I was growing impatient.

"Ty, give me a break! I told you she was my best friend; we tell each other everything! You don't have to worry, it's not like Karena has a big mouth or anything. She's not one of those girls who run their mouths all the time."

"A characteristic you two obviously don't share!"

Okay, now he didn't have to go there! Was he losin' his damn mind or something?

"Ty, I think that was a bit uncalled for," I said through clinched teeth.

He pushed me off him and started to get dressed.

"Look Yaniya, it's late and I gotta work in the morning."

What the hell?! I know this dude ain't rollin' out on me!

I had to turn the sweetness back on. I sat up on my knees and rubbed my breasts together, trying to tease him so that he would stay and get back to grubbin'.

"Oh Ty, come on now. *We* know you want to stay. Don't you wanna play with us?"

Ty looked at me and stopped all movement. His eyes said he wanted me and he licked his lips hungrily.

Hook, line, and sinker! Come on back to Mama!

He walked over to me, kissed two of his fingers then held them up to my lips.

"As tempting as you, um, ya'll are, I'ma have to pass."

This time, I couldn't hide my anger.

"No the hell you didn't come all the way over here, start eatin' my pussy, and now your 'bout to leave just because you're salty over me tellin' my girl you were here and what we were doin'?! What the fuck difference does it make if I told her or not? It's after midnight; you think she thought you and I were over here havin' a fuckin' Blockbuster night?"

Ty shook his head and laughed. That mothafucka was actually standin' up in *my* house, after just gettin' outta *my* bed, and laughin' at me! What was the damn punch line?

"Look, I'll holla back."

I flipped over onto my back and did a spread eagle; all my glistening womanhood was exposed in his face.

"The least you could do is to go back down there so I can get satisfied!"

Ty chuckled again before walking out the door.

No the fuck he didn't!

Reggie

Thanksgiving was approaching and I was going to spend the holiday with Karena and her family in Ohio. I know my parents were kind of upset that I was choosing to spend my first holiday out with her and her people as opposed to them, but I could see my family anytime. Karena and I had to cherish the few times we have to spend together, until she moved here that is.

I was anxious to see what her people were going to think about me; I wondered if she had told them I had been incarcerated and if so, did she provide them with the horrid details?

My Pops and I finally had a long talk about Karena and the relationship we were trying to establish.

It was a typical Saturday at the Compton house: Rodney and some of his friends were in his room plastered to the TV playing basketball on the Play Station III; Mom was out running errands and shopping with Karena's cousin Ryan, and Pops was holding himself hostage in his office on the phone, making sure all the business was right. I was in my own world drawing in my sketchbook. I loved to draw and was good at it if I say so myself. I probably would've gone to an Art school or something, but I had devoted my time to the wrong things and my talent was put on the back burner.

"Reggie, we need to talk," Pops voice boomed. "Come on into my office."

I walked into the office and sat down in one of the black leather chairs. Pops was sitting behind his mahogany desk but got up and positioned himself in the other chair facing me.

He poured himself a glass of Crown Royal and lit a Cuban cigar. I straightened up in my seat; this was gonna be serious. Pops only drunk Crown Royal and smoked Cubans when he had something heavy on his mind. Like when I first got down here and we had our talk about what I wanted to do with my life now that I was out. Before I even sat down, he was already sippin' and puffin'. The Cuban cigars, they were so smooth and mellow, just like Pops. He kept them in a platinum case under the baseboard of the bottom locked drawer of his desk and didn't share with anyone. Don't ask me how he got them; let's just say Calvin had connections.

"So, what did you wanna talk about?" I asked.

He took a hit of the Cuban and gangsta-leaned back in the chair.

"What's goin' on with you and Karena?"

"We're trying to make things happen."

"So, give me some particulars."

"Well, to be honest, I told her I was in love with her and that I wanted to get married."

Pops started choking on his cigar and laughed heartily.

"You told her what?"

"Come on Pops, I know you heard me."

"Boy, you ain't been outta prison but a hot minute! You just met the girl, now you ready to marry her?" Pops wiped his tearing eyes. "Man to Man Reggie: is that her sugar bowl talkin'? It has been a while for you; are you sure it's not the sex that's bringing you to the conclusion of marriage?"

Damn, I was very insulted! My own father was treating me like I'm some hard-up-for-a-fuck loser! Shit, I had had plenty of good pussy in my day and still managed to keep my focus!

"That's a fucked up thing to say, Pops!" I told him.

He saw the seriousness in my face and stopped laughing.

"Okay, my fault for laughing. On the real tip, are you seriously considering marriage? That's a big step and the girl ain't even moved down here yet! What does she have to say about all this?"

"Look, I have done a lot of bad things up to this point."

"You ain't neva lied!" He cracked.

"Can I finish? Like I was saying, I've done many bad things up to this point, but I finally have my head on straight and part of that is because of Karena. She encourages me; she talks to me and lets me know that she'll be there for me when I need her. No girl I've ever messed with made me feel that type of realness, and I'm not about to mess things up with her!"

"Son, I'm not saying you two can't be together. I'm glad you finally met someone who cares about you and is not judging you from your past mistakes. I see the way you act whenever she's around or you talk about her, and I can tell you really do care for her. You've been through a lot of bad things, but now a lot of good is coming out of it. All I'm saying is that maybe you guys should just take your time, court for a while and then get married in a year or two."

"Did you think we were gonna do it tomorrow?"

Pops sighed and swallowed the rest of his drink while I continued.

"By the way, Karena is cool with the idea of getting married. She's in love with me and for the first time I know it's real. And we are going to take our time; I just wanted her to know what my plans were."

"So, Karena's the one huh?"

"She is the one and only!"

Pops said, "Man, I remember the first time I saw Janine; 1976 Louisville. I had pulled into this gas station. She was walkin' across the parking lot and I thought to myself 'Damn, now there goes a real woman!' She had on this strapless sundress and these high-heeled shoes. Her hair was much longer back then, flowed way down her back and she had a white headband around it. She was just a young thing back then, too. Hell, she even had a boyfriend."

"I thought ya'll were both single when you guys met."

"Naw, only I was single. You know your dad was a big ol' pimp back in the day, I couldn't be tied down with just one!"

Here we go! Wasn't everybody's dad a self-proclaimed pimp way back when? Although with my pops, that idea wasn't hard to believe.

"Anyway, I laid eyes on her and it was like she had stepped into a spotlight; I couldn't focus on nothin' else! I swear I even heard harps playin' and shit, like I had just entered the pearly gates or somethin'!"

I started howlin'! That's probably the only time he'd get close to the pearly gates!

"I walked right over to her, her man was mean- muggin' the hell outta me too, and I introduced myself. I told her I thought she was a vision of beauty and that one day we were gonna get married."

"What did she say?" I was cracking up!

"Nothing at first because her man came rollin' up on me like he was 'bout to start some shit. You know me; I kept my cool and kept right on talkin'. Told her that when she got tired of playin' with her "boyfriend", I'd be there to pick up where he left off and we'd get married."

"And what did she say?"

"She looked at dude, looked back at me and said," he made his voice very high, mocking my mom, "I'm tired of playing with him, so what did you say your name was again?"

We both fell out laughing.

"Six months later we were married and six *weeks* later she was pregnant with you."

"See, you guys had only known each other for six months! Why are you making such a big deal about me and Karena?"

He stroked his mustache and beard.

"It was a different time then, Son. You didn't spend a lot of time going out on dates before proposing and eventually getting married. It was love at first sight, for both of us and we still to this day believe that it was our destiny to be together. I didn't need to get gas that day; something or someone," he said pointing above, "Told me to pull into that station and there she was."

"So what are you sayin'; can that not be the same thing going on with me and Karena? Can't my destiny be to have a life with her and vice versa?"

"You've got a point. I'm not trying to discourage you Reggie; I know it may sound like that. It would be great if you two could share what your mother and I shared. That sort of thing doesn't happen very often anymore, not in this day in age. Just remember what I told you: take your time. If it's meant to be then it will be."

Two weeks later, I was still thinking about the conversation I'd had with Pops. I truly believed meeting Karena had been fate and I intended to do what I had to do to make our relationship grow.

It was Thanksgiving and I was in Ohio. The city was beautiful and Karena's neighborhood looked like some kind of fall advertisement; most of the leaves had already changed colors and had fallen all over the place! Some kids where outside running and jumping into huge piles of leaves while others were raking and bagging them up.

Every so often, a car or two would pull up in front of the houses and people would pour out of them and carry their covered dishes inside. It seemed like the whole block smelled like a soul food restaurant and my stomach growled continuously!

The Murphy residence was filled to the rim with people! I tried to be cool while I was introduced to this cousin or that aunt, but I was very nervous.

Eventually I ended up in the kitchen. Once her family found out I helped manage a restaurant Karena's Aunt Jane came, whisked me away from my comfortable seat in the living room's overstuffed chair, and into the kitchen to help. She handed me a white apron that read, "You wish you could cook like me". Amari and Karena's mom Lynn were already in there preparing macaroni and cheese and the sweet potato pie filling. My mouth started watering!

"You might as well wash up those hands and get to helpin'." Aunt Jane said. Jane was one of the aunts on Ms. Lynn's side. She was a brown skin short and plump woman with a short bob haircut. I could tell right away that she was the aunt who bossed everyone around, but it was cool. She had me cracking up, telling stories about Karena when she was younger.

"You know Reggie; it's a good thing K got her act together otherwise, you probably wouldn't have gotten a chance to meet her." I was helping Aunt Jane make candied yams, one of my favorites.

"Why is that, Aunt Jane?"

"Well, because she woulda been dead! Karena used to have a mouth on her that woulda made the Lord himself wanna come down here and snatch her behind up from her roots!"

I died laughin'! Karena walked in and playfully poked her aunt.

"Aunt J, I wasn't that bad!"

"Humph, you keep livin' in that fantasy! I'm just glad the good Lord gave us all the strength to keep dealin' with you, 'cause you know it was only His grace that saved you from a few beat downs."

Karena grabbed my arm and started dragging me out of the kitchen.

"Come on baby, I want you to meet my Grandma Mae."

"No," I said chuckling, "I think I want to stay in here with Aunt Jane and talk about you some more."

"I don't think you do! Let's go!"

I felt my nervousness coming back on. Grandma Mae was the family matriarch; she was like a Don in a mafia family. I went over to the sink to wash my hands and gave my borrowed apron back to Ms. Lynn. I wanted to go into the bathroom to make sure I still looked alright, but Karena insisted I was good to go.

"Baby, you look fine. Don't be nervous, my Grandma is cool peeps and she's been dying to meet you."

We walked into the living room and there she was; Grandma Mae looked like a typical grandmother. She was short and round, dark skinned with tinted glasses, and shoulder-length curly gray hair.

"So, you must be the Reggie I've been hearin' so much about?"

"Yes ma'am, Reggie Compton."

We hugged. She smelled like Oscar de la Renta perfume.

"Well, it's nice to meet you. I'm Grandma Mae, but you can call me Big Mama."

"Okay, Big Mama do you have any stories about Karena when she was little?"

"Humph, chile Karena ain't neva been little!" Big Mama giggled and Karena held her hand up over her eyes. I could tell she was embarrassed by the comment, so I kissed her on the check and held her around her waist.

"Karena was really a delightful child," Big Mama continued. "She just got to her teenage years and turned into a heathen, like most of ya'll do."

"I think I'ma go see if they need any more help in the kitchen," Karena said.

The rest of the day flew by and I had loved every minute of it. It was like I had been stuck in a whirlwind cross between a restaurant commercial and a primetime soap opera; my head was spinning by the time Karena and I returned to her north side apartment.

I met more family members than I could count, or remember for that matter. I ate so much that my stomach was pokin' out like I was pregnant! We had ham, cranberry sauce, turkey and stuffing, greens, macaroni and cheese, mashed potatoes and gravy, a pound cake, and three kinds of pie: apple, sweet potato, and pumpkin.

Everyone was so nice to me and treated me like I'd known them for years! I did miss being around my own family though, playin' football with my uncles and cousins, then watching a game on TV. I was definitely gonna miss my Aunt Katie's bread pudding, which always was the first thing to get demolished! My two cousins, Lamar and YaYa and I would always argue over the last serving of it and I always ended up winning. I had such a great time at the Murphy house anyway; and being with Karena was just a bonus and made the day that much more perfect.

That Saturday Karena took me on a little tour of Columbus. We enjoyed some first-thing-in-the-morning lovemaking, slept in a bit, then got

dressed and hit the streets. Karena's Ford Explorer

was nice and toasty inside, a welcomed change

from the frosty city air. The maroon truck was

showroom-new clean and smelled like watermelon

Jolly Ranchers.

We were off!

Karena drove like she was late for a meeting

with the President or something! She dipped and

dived her way in between cars and turned corners so

quick that I thought we would end up on two

wheels!

"Baby, do you moonlight as a racecar

driver?" I asked her while clutching the door.

"Why, am I goin' a little too fast for ya?"

"Just a bit," I said, making sure my seatbelt

was nice and tight.

We jumped on 71 south and didn't look back. She showed me all the schools she'd gone to, where she worked, the best mall and movie theaters, the Columbus Museum of Art, and all over the downtown area. We stopped at B J's Mongolian Barbeque to have lunch, even though we had all those leftovers back at her crib, then walked up and down High Street's Short North area galleries and looked at the different art. The day was perfect!

Sunday we went to Karena's church, but during the service, all I thought about was how much I wanted to be in between her thighs! It was my last day there and later that night I was headed back to Georgia. I didn't know how many times we had sex since I got into town, but I wanted to put it on her in the worse way at the most inappropriate time!

I looked over at Karena; her gray V-neck sweater showed a small amount of her cleavage and her breasts rose up and down with her breathing. I got a woody right then and there and imagined myself sucking her nipples, all while the Minister was preaching about fornication!

"Karena, I think I need to step out," I whispered.

"Why, is everything okay?"

"No, I'm about to bust out of my pants."

She looked down at the bulge I was so desperately trying to battle.

"Oh, I see," She chuckled. "It's almost over baby, so try to think about golf or something."

By the time the benediction came, I had blue balls the size of my damn head! Karena introduced me to some people, including the pastor and his wife. At the time, I was thinking to myself, "I could give a flyin' fuck about who you are!" and I had to hold my jacket over my pants the whole time.

Karena had been feeling the heat too because she did about ninety on the freeway with her hand inside my boxers and stroked me all the way back to her house. She had my shirt unbuttoned and I had her stockings and panties halfway down before we even got inside her building. I was hoping that nobody saw us, but I really didn't care!

We threw our coats down as soon as we entered her apartment and tore at each other like lovers who would have only one last chance to be together.

I took my shirt off and Karena kissed all over my chest. I pulled her panties completely off, lifted one of her legs up and tickled the inside of her pussy with two of my fingers.

I snatched off her sweater and bra and flung them across the room. Her dark nipples stood at attention while I swirled my tongue around each one.

"Reggie, I want you inside me baby!"

Karena faced the wall and hiked her skirt up higher. My pants had been kicked over to the side somewhere, but my boxers never made it passed my ankles. I pulled her farther from the wall and bent her over. I entered her from behind and went to work! .

Karena had one hand up against the wall and the other on my ass, guiding me in and out of her. We might as well have been in an alley up against a pole!

"Grab your ankles," I commanded.

Say what you will about big girls, but they really know how to take the dick! She bent over some more and did as she was told. She arched her back and I tightly held onto her waist so she wouldn't fall. The sound of our skin slapping up against each other drowned out our moans and cuss words.

I felt my legs tensing up and the sweat from my body dropped onto Karena and rolled down her back. I could feel an orgasm coming on and the sensation made me thrust into her harder and faster.

"Yes Reggie!"

Karena somehow managed to match my speed and rhythm; she put her hands right above her knees and rolled her ass in circles around my dick;

once again, we were in sync. I stood still while she popped up and down.

"Gatdamn, you feel good, Karena! Is this my pussy?"

"Oh yes, it's yours baby! It's all yours!"

"Tell me this pussy belongs to me!"

"This pussy belongs to only you, Reggie!"

"Oh shit, oh shit!"

I felt a jolt and it was almost like I had been jumpin' up and down inside of Karena. It was the most exhilarating orgasm I'd ever had; I had to hold onto the wall for support. We never made it pass the doorway!

Eventually we ended up in her room and collapsed on the bed. It suddenly occurred to me that I hadn't used a condom.

"Baby, are you on the pill?" I nervously asked her.

"Nope," She said nonchalantly.

"We didn't use anything."

"I know."

"And I came inside you."

"I know that, too."

"I just got so carried away and felt so good…"

"I liked the way it felt, your seeds spilling into me."

"I liked the way it felt too, but what if you get pregnant?"

"Baby, don't worry about it. I'm very in tune with my body and this is not my fertile period."

Karena spread her legs and I climbed in between them and placed my head on her chest. She put her arms around me we held each other. I rose up and kissed her lightly on the lips. We lay together like that until we couldn't let any more time pass and I absolutely had to leave.

Yaniya

So, I finally got a chance to meet Reggie and I must admit I was rather surprised. I mean, it's not like my girl had bad taste in men or anything, but she did sometimes seem to attract the unattractive: thugs, wanna-be gangstas, and GED rejects.

I was expecting a ghetto-ass, countrified dude that had nappy braids and a raggedy mouth full of gold teeth. However, Reggie was sweet, very attentive towards Karena, respectful, and sexy as hell! His clothes were neat, his pants weren't hanging off his ass, and his kicks were crispy white!

She brought him by my place his first night in town. Ty had since forgiven me after our little tiff and we all decided to go out to eat at this place called "The Melting Pot", a classy restaurant that specialized in fondue and all kinds of wines and champagnes.

You could tell Reggie was an old fashion type of guy: he opened doors for Karena, ushered her in and out of the car, held her hand when we walked, the whole nine! He even dipped her strawberries in the melted chocolate and fed them to her! They were all over each other the whole time, sharing little kisses here and there, and hanging on each other's every word!

I was rather annoyed to tell you the truth; I can't stand that all that mushy shit! Regardless of that, Ty hardly acted like he even wanted to be with me! It was like we were just pals, maybe even brother and sister because he wouldn't touch me, not even to hold my hand or nothing!

At the very least, he did open the door and pull out my chair for me, but that ain't shit! He's supposed to do those things! He didn't try to cuddle up to me, much less feed me a damn strawberry! He barely talked to me at all, he was too busy drilling Reggie with questions about Atlanta and wondering about Karena's plans.

"Karena, when do you think you'll be moving?" Ty asked.

"I'd like to know the answer to that myself," Reggie said.

"Well, I talked to Ryan and I've decided to move right after Christmas so that I can kick off the New Year in my new city," Karena replied.

Reggie kissed her and Ty offered his congratulations. I tried to be happy for Karena, but all I could think about was the fact that I was losing my best friend. Georgia was so fucking far away!

Plus, she never once even asked me if I wanted to

move with her and that really stung! I could've

gotten my own apartment so it's not like I would've

begged to live with her and her cousins. It was

merely the principal of the matter.

"Right after Christmas, huh? That's only a

month away, so I guess you better hurry up and start

packing." I tried to disguise the hurt in my voice. I

hope it worked!

"Girl please, I started packin' the minute I

got the green light from Ryan. I can't wait to be up

outta here!" Karena said.

Damn, did she have to make it sound like

Columbus was the absolute worst place to live?

"And guess what else?" She continued.

"Ryan thought it would be a good idea if I invited a

friend or two to come down and bring in the New Year with me. The weekend would include roundtrip airfare and a room in a slammin' hotel in downtown ATL, courtesy of Mr. Juan Ramirez. Now, I wonder; what two fine individuals could I invite?"

Ty and I looked at each other, then back at Karena.

"Hey Reggie, you're going to meet several of my peeps this weekend. Perhaps you could help me decide what two people would be deserving of a free weekend in the ATL." Karena teased.

I shot her a don't-mess-with-me look and she and Reggie cracked up.

"Of course I want you and Ty to come! I just had to make you sweat a little bit!" She assured.

"Thanks for the invite, Karena! There was no way in the world would I miss spending New Year's in Atlanta!" Ty exclaimed.

A weekend in Atlanta and I wouldn't have to pay for a thing! All those New Year's Eve parties; oh, the trouble I could get myself into swimming in a Georgia cesspool of sin, sex, alcohol, and men I'd never see again.

I wish Karena hadn't of mentioned this in front of Ty. He was cool to hang out with around *this* city, but there was no way in hell I was going to parade him around as my man while we were in Atlanta. I was trying to find me some fresh meat down there; a nice weekend fling, you know, for creating holiday memories.

Karena and I excused ourselves to the restroom. There were two tacky looking girls inside applying cheap, corner store lipstick to their already clown made-up faces. They looked at us, made a face, and walked out trailing the stench of too much designer imposter perfume. I started gagging.

"Damn, did they have to pour on the whole bottle? Anyway, thanks for the invite to the dirty dirty, girl. But why did you have to invite Ty to come along?"

Karena was touching up her Fashion Fair cocoa lipstick.

"I thought he was your man?"

"I never said all that!"

"But that's how you act. Anytime Ty doesn't appear to be at your disposal you start clocking. Besides, I don't know of any other guys you're dating."

When you don't want someone to know the real deal about a situation, what else is there to do besides put on a front?

"First of all: I do not need Ty to be at my beck and call, so there's no need to clock about anything! Secondly, you don't have to know all the guys I'm dating. Ty just happens to be the one I like the most, that's all."

"But since when don't we tell each other our business?" Karena mocked.

"Damn, I fell right into that one! Let's go!"

When I got home, I immediately starting making a list of the things I would need to do before my big New Year's weekend. I had to get a new outfit, make sure my hair was as smooth as butter, and get my NaNa waxed; not many guys liked a hairy coochie.

Of course, I would have to pack the clothes that made my body look even more perfect than it already was. I also had to make sure that I had only my cutest matching panties and bras and maybe even some lingerie; a girl should always be prepared!

I had to call my mom to tell her about my plans. She and my stepdad, Jacob Smallwood was planning to come for Christmas and stay up through New Year's Day. I was going to go visit them for Thanksgiving, but at the last minute Jacob had to go on some business trip that he couldn't get out of. My mom and I could've hung out together, but she decided to stay stuck up under him instead.

Don't get me wrong; I did miss my mom and my stepdad was cool. But they were going to have to leave before my trip. I wasn't missing that for the world!

My mother is a paralegal and when the attorney she was working for got a promotion as a senior partner at a prestigious law firm in Chicago, he wanted her to come with him. It was the summer before my senior year in high school and at the time, I wasn't ready to leave Columbus, believe it or not. I didn't want to graduate from a different school and be away from my friends, but my mom had to leave right away.

We agreed that I would stay with my Godmother and her daughter until I turned eighteen, then I could move out into my own apartment. Mom said she would help me with my expenses as long as I continued to make good grades when I enrolled in college, which I did. I've been on my own ever since.

Just as I was about to pick up the phone, it rang. It was Jacob.

"Hey Yaniya, how are you?"

"Hey Jacob, what's shakin'?"

Jacob was six-four, a solid 245, and had the most beautiful gray eyes. He's a litigator with the firm my mom works at and they started dating not long after she moved there.

Jacob was loaded: he and my mother lived in a nice condo and both of them drove a Bens.

He wanted to buy me a car for my twenty-first birthday, but my mom talked him out of it. So instead, he gave me the down payment for one I could afford on my own and he paid the insurance on it for a year! He was nice to me and always treated me like I was his daughter, not just his stepdaughter. He also treated my mom like a queen! I could tell he really loved and respected her, something that was extremely important to me.

"I'm doing great, thanks. I just wanted to call and apologize for us not being able to spend Thanksgiving together," He said regretfully.

"It's cool Jacob; I understand that you have business to take care of. I'll be cool and will probably be chilling with Karena and her people."

That was a lie. I knew Karena would be spending the holiday with Reggie and introducing him to the family. I didn't want to be a third wheel for that, sitting up under them while they were all over each other. No thanks!

My biological father and his side of the family lived here, but I didn't want to be around them. I never felt like I was welcomed any of the other times I had gone to see them; it was like they just tolerated my presence because of my dad. Besides, my father and I did not have the best relationship anyway, so I was cool.

"Well, as long as you're not going to be alone. That right there is the only reason why I didn't suggest you come along with us; you're mom thought you would be bored to tears," Jacob said.

Like she would know or even care, I thought to myself.

My mother and I could've spent time together while Jacob tended to his business, but nooo! She wouldn't dare do a silly thing like spend some quality time with me, which would almost be like doing the right thing!

"Don't worry about it," I told him. "I'm glad you called because I was just about to call you guys. I wanted to talk about the Christmas plans."

"Hold on Yaniya, your mother wants to speak to you," He interrupted.

I heard some jingling around before my mom, Anitra got on the phone.

"Hey Niya, how are you baby?" My mom sounded unusually chipper.

"I'm really good, Ma. You sound good, so how are you feelin?"

"Oh, I feel wonderful! I just left the spa; Jacob surprised me with a gift certificate for a full day of rest and relaxation at this place called "Easy Street". It was heavenly."

I could definitely use a day at the spa. I really didn't want to hear her rant and rave about her day on Easy Street, so I quickly got to the point.

"That's great to hear Ma. Listen, I wanted to talk to you about Christmas. I know you and Jacob were gonna come and…"

"Well baby that might be a problem," She said, suddenly not sounding so damn chipper.

She continued, "You see, Jacob's parents had invited us to spend the holidays with them. I had already accepted before I remembered that we were supposed to be coming there to visit you. Honey, I'm sorry."

I could feel my blood boiling! How could she forget that she was supposed to spend one of the most important holidays of the year with her only child? I really wanted to be with her, so I tried to compromise.

"Okay, so why don't I come with you? It's been forever since I've seen Grandma and Grandpa Smallwood. I would have to leave a little early, but I'm sure they wouldn't mind."

Silence.

"Well I thought about that, but they live in a small town in Louisiana now and you know how you hate the country, so I didn't arrange a ticket for you. The last thing I'd want is to hear you whining and complaining about how they don't have this luxury or that the whole time. You know how materialistic you can be, Yaniya."

Now I was livid! My own mother was playing me!

"Mom, I'm not that materialistic! If I don't see you guys this year, who knows when it'll be before we get another chance. You know as soon as the holidays are over the firm will be bombarded with cases!"

"I'm sorry honey, but I promise you that we will get together soon after the New Year. We'll have our own spa day, go shopping, the works!"

I could've hung up on her! So not only was I not going to be able to see my mother for Thanksgiving, I wasn't going to see her over Christmas or New Year's either! She didn't even try to meet me halfway on a solution or seem the least bit upset.

I wanted to cry and beg her to come see me, but I didn't want to give her the satisfaction of knowing I was hurt. She would've only used that as ammo for her next attack. I did the only thing I knew how to do better than anything else; I acted like I didn't give a fuck!

"You know what, Ma? It's cool because I have new plans of my own. I'm going to Atlanta with Karena and another friend of ours, that's what I wanted to tell you. So have a happy turkey day. And if I don't talk to you then, have a Merry Christmas and a Happy New Year, too!"

I hung up before she could get a word in.

Karena

It was three in the morning when I heard the phone ring.

I was finally in Atlanta for good; my mother and I drove my car down and my brother and father followed behind us in a U-Haul. On this particular occasion, I was spending the night with Reggie in his new, two-bedroom apartment in Clarkston, about fifteen minutes or so away from his parents' house.

It was clearly a bachelor pad: everything from the blinds to the furniture to the carpeting was either beige or dark brown. Reggie loved dark colors and had matching black and blue towels, washcloths, bath mats, sheets and pillowcases; you name it!

We had just finished having some of the best mind-blowing sex, just a hair shy of it being a porno movie. Reggie ate me out for over thirty minutes and I had cum so many times that I lost count! We did the sixty-nine, (him on top of course 'cause I didn't wanna smash the poor boy!) and after we both exploded in each other's mouths, we drifted into a deep, coma-like sleep.

The phone's ringer must have been up on high, because when the phone rung I almost jumped up out of the bed. This was the third time somebody had called here this late when I was staying over. Reggie only stirred slightly, but the second ring got his attention. He yanked his arm out from under me and grabbed the phone.

"Who the fuck is it?" He yelled into the receiver.

As I made a mental note never to wake him up outta his sleep, he turned his back to me and his voice got softer and almost seemed to fade away. I mean, I was lying right beside him but couldn't hear a word he was saying. I thought I made out something like, 'why you callin' here this damn late'? or something, but I wasn't for sure. It also occurred to me that he had done the same thing the other times when the phone rang late at night.

I lied there motionless, but not pretending to be sleep. Reggie hung up the phone and rubbed his head like something was troubling him. He slightly turned his head my way to see if I was still asleep.

"No, I'm not sleep," I let him know.

"Sorry I woke you up, baby. I can get kinda rough when I'm ripped outta my sleep."

He bent down and kissed me, then flipped back over in an attempt to return to sleep. I immediately got an attitude. *Was he serious?* I know he didn't think I was about to let that shit slide! Somebody, obviously a female, calls my man's house in the middle of the fuckin' night and he has the nerve to act all nonchalant about it!

"Um, excuse me Reggie?" I said, sitting up in the bed.

He turned over and seemed to be surprised that I was not asleep.

"What's wrong?"

"Are you for real? Did your phone not just ring at fuckin' three in the morning, again? Please don't try to play me 'cause I know that was a girl on the phone!"

Reggie sighed and sat up in the bed. He went to turn on the light, but I pulled his hand down. I didn't want him to look at me, to see the hurt that was masked by my fierceness.

"I'm sorry about that. Look, it's not what you think. That was some broad I messed with the first couple of days I got outta prison. She asked my cousin Buster for my number and he gave it to her"

"Damn, so what number am I? You were only outta prison for a few weeks when we met, and I thought you said it had been a while since you got any?"

"I said it had been a while since I had some pussy and I was tellin' you the truth! That broad just sucked my dick, that's all! I made it clear at the time that I only wanted some head, but she was tryin' to get me to be her man."

"Does she know about me? If she does, maybe I should check her ass because she's being awfully disrespectful right now."

"Of course she knows about you! And even if there were no you I still wouldn't want her!"

I have to admit, hearing him say that did make me feel a little better about the situation, but I was still pissed. Reggie was looking at me like he was pleading with me to believe him. I didn't wanna argue with him or seem like I would never give him the benefit of the doubt, so I decided to drop it, for the time being.

I kissed him and said, "I'm sorry I started trippin'. Let's just go back to sleep."

"Karena, we said we'd always be honest with each other. I don't plan to renege on that."

Reggie put his arms back around me and we lay as we did before, but something was different. The pot of doubt concerning our relationship had begun to simmer and I didn't know if it could be turned off.

New Year's Eve had come and I was ready to partay! Niya and Ty were in town and I had spent most of the day with them. Of course, Reggie was working and we were all going to meet up at his family's restaurant for their big New Year's Eve party.

After we had decided on what slammin' outfits we'd be decked out in, I took my guests from their posh downtown Atlanta Hilton hotel room to Ryan and Juan's suburban oasis for some pre-party drinking'.

It seemed like all the freeways were stacked; you could only imagine what the destinations were for the passengers inside the vehicles. We were sitting at the light on Wesley Chapel Road and Snapfinger when a 1990 Oldsmobile Cutlass pulled up beside us. There had to be about seven people stuffed into that bad boy! They were playing "Player's Anthem" by Outcast.

The passenger side window slid down and there was so much smoke coming out of it that the car looked like it was on fire! It was evident that some serious weed was being smoked.

"Hey, where ya'll peeps headed?" The driver hollered. He had on red and green headbands around his wild 'fro, being festive for the holidays I guess.

Ty put his window down and hollered from the backseat, "We rollin' down to that place Compton and Company for their party later on."

"That's where I want to go!" The girl sitting in the middle pouted.

"Ya'll need to be at the New Year's cabaret over on Memorial at the Ramada; that's 'bout to be off the hook!" The driver yelled.

Homeboy asked the girl on the passenger's side to pass a flier to me through the open windows. Although I had no intentions of going, I took it anyway and yelled, "Thanks, we might shoot through."

"It's gonna be hot! Ya'll be safe and have a good night!" Passenger girl said. The rest of the group screamed their "Happy New Year's" and pulled off.

Car systems bumped their 808's and every stoplight held a different musical medley then the one before. People just seemed to be ready to have a good time, and I was one of those who could not wait to cut a rug!

At the Ramirez's humble abode, Ty and Juan played pool and talked sports while we women gossiped and put the finishing touches on our already fired up attire.

"Damn!" Ryan cursed.

She had just fastened the last button on her flared blue jeans. Her red, off the shoulder sweater showed an ample amount of cleavage, but not too much to where she'd be poppin' out all over the place. She had one diamond earring dangling from her ear and was frantically searching for its twin, pushing aside all the others in her mahogany jewelry box.

"I know Gabby has been in here! I don't know how many times I've told that girl to stay outta my jewelry box!" Ryan stormed out of the room and returned a minute later with the missing accessory. She zipped up her red ankle boots, grabbed her blue jean jacket and red Kangol and gave Niya and me thumbs up.

We had all decided to dress casually for the evening. I was down for that because I wanted no restrictions on me gettin' my groove on tonight! I chose my black sparkled jeans and matching jacket. Juan had on a blue jean outfit that matched Ryan's, (some couples are so sickening!) and Ty had on a pair of Khakis with a red and tan Atlanta Braves embroidered shirt.

Everybody was going to wear some type of hat: I matched my cuz and wore my black Kangol; Ty wore a circa-1986 LL Cool J bucket hat, and Juan sported a red baseball cap.

Niya was the only one who strayed from our casual theme: she was wearing a short, spaghetti-strapped, silver slinky dress that had the nerve to have slits on both sides that came all the way up her thighs, as if it didn't show enough already! He boobs were pouring out all over the place and I was sure that by the end of the night they would tumble out.

Nobody said anything while she sashayed all over the house. Ryan looked annoyed and I was almost ashamed to have invited her into my family's home, but I felt it was best to let it go. I didn't want to have an attitude and mess up everyone else's evening. Besides, as I said before, some things were better left unsaid.

Ty was obviously bothered by her wardrobe choice, because when she came twirling out of the bathroom at the hotel he just looked at her and shook his head in disgust.

"What, don't I look good Ty?" Niya asked sweetly. She just did that out of spite; she knew Ty wasn't going to like her dress. He nodded and walked out the door and Niya chuckled to herself.

"Why you actin' like that, Niya? You know good and well what he thinks about that dress! It doesn't leave much to the imagination, you know," I scolded.

"Of course I know; that's exactly why I'm wearing it. Girl, we're in Atlanta and its New

Year's Eve, so gimme a break! Ty's feelings ain't hurt, and if they are I'm sure he'll get over it!"

Niya must have thought she had Ty wrapped around her little finger, but I had a feeling that he was beginning to get tired of the way she treated him.

I was on my second shot of Hennessy and feelin' mighty nice by the time we were all ready to head over to the party. We jumped into Juan's GMC Denali and off we went.

There were so many damn people at the restaurant! You could hear the music all the way down the street and people were walking, laughing and joking their way to the crowded restaurant. There was even a line for the valet; some people just gave up, did a U-turn and decided to park the car themselves somewhere else.

Once we were inside, we checked our jackets and started mingling. Everybody was in the holiday spirit, drinking and dancing. People I'd never seen before in my life came up to me and offered hugs and greetings like we went way back.

The white linen and fancy dishes and cutlery were replaced by red and green tablecloths. Little silver Happy New Year sprinkles dusted the tabletops. A buffet was set up and had an array of good eats: meatballs, clam dip, cheese, meat, and relish trays, fried mozzarella sticks, and plenty of fresh fruit. At the end of the table was a variety of soft drinks and juices, plus a wait staff carried trays of champagne around and the bar was open in case something stronger was desired.

I spotted Reggie at the bar. Damn, he was looking good enough to eat in his striped shirt, white tee and baggy jeans. He had a fresh haircut and shave and I knew he was wearing his Gucci cologne, my favorite.

Reggie was talking to some girl, or shall I say the girl was talking to him. He really didn't seem that interested, even though she was trying to work all her angles to get his attention. I stood there and watched; that tramp was runnin' her hand up and down my man's chest!

She was sitting on a bar stool, her short skirt was hiked up even more to show off her thick legs. Her breasts seemed to be screaming for mercy from the clutches of her way too tight, low-cut sleeveless shirt and she traced the lining of her exposed chest seductively.

I waited for Reggie to push her hand away, put her in her place. The longer I waited the more I realized he was continuing to let her hands explore

him. I'm sure smoke could be seen coming out of

my head because I was burnin' up! I put my hands

on my hips and sucked my teeth.

Ryan and Niya came up behind me and

noticed my heated glare towards the bar. Niya

handed me a drink.

"Who the fuck is that?!" She bellowed.

"Her name is Kima Brown," Ryan

answered. "She's a waitress and bartender here."

"Why she got her hands all over my girl's

man?" Niya asked.

"I think the better question should be why

my man is allowing her to have her hands all over

him?!" I spat out.

I felt like a chump standing there while

Reggie was flirting with some other girl. They were

all up on each other. Didn't he know I was gonna be here?

"Kima is somethin' else," Ryan said. "She's wanted Reggie since he first got down here and has tried her hardest to hook him, too. But don't worry Karena; everyone knows how he feels about you."

"She's right, girl," Niya added. "Just look at her; she's practically throwing herself at him, lookin' all cheap and shit! Look at that raggedy weave! She could've at least hot curled the ends or somethin'.

Kima had a red-highlighted weave that was silky smooth in the front and on the side, but wickedly untamed in the back. I started laughing and Niya hugged my shoulders. It was moments like this that made me remember why she was my girl.

"Kima is like school on a Sunday: no class!" Ryan said. "Why don't you go over there and show her where Reggie's interests really lie?"

Drink in hand, I pushed my way through the crowed and over to the bar. I wasn't about to let either of them see how mad I was, so hid my attitude, took a sip of my drink, and tapped Reggie on the shoulder. He turned around and it was clear that he was caught off guard. He finally pushed home girl's hand away and kissed me.

"Hey baby, I didn't think you'd be here so early," He yelled over the loud music.

"I can see that. Aren't you gonna introduce me to your little friend?"

He turned back to the girl and said, "Karena, this is Kima. She works here. Kima, this is my lady Karena."

Kima shifted in her seat and pulled her skirt down. She folded her arms and had the nerve to look me up and down!

"Wassup, Karena?" She said with a smirk.

No this bitch was not smirking at me!

I could've slapped her ass right off the damn stool! As furious as I was, I managed to stay cool.

"I'm just here to have a good time and bring in the New Year with my man. Come on, baby let's dance." I pulled Reggie away from Ms. Hot Pants before she could say a word. Maybe that would cool her ass off!

The D J took it back and Babyface's "Whip Appeal" blasted all through the building. Dozens of couples flooded the dance floor and began swaying back and forth with the tempo, holding tightly to one another.

Reggie and I spotted Ryan and Juan all snuggly with each other as we took the floor and copied everyone else. Ryan winked at me as Reggie and I embraced. I looked around for Yaniya but I didn't spot her. I did however see Ty dancing with a short, dark skinned woman. She was gazing up into his eyes and they were dancing closely. Nothing about Ty's expression told me that he cared one iota about where Niya was.

Reggie noticed Ty with the shorty and asked, "Does Yaniya know her man is all up on another woman? They're dancing awfully close."

"I hope she's in a corner somewhere watching them," I said harshly. "I know Niya is just playin' him. She really doesn't treat him like he's her man. And anyway, weren't you all up on somebody when I walked in?"

"Karena, don't start," Reggie sighed.

"What do mean, 'Karena don't start'? I mocked. "You gonna stand there and tell me that you weren't all over that Kima girl!"

"No, I wasn't all over her; she was all over me."

"Yes I noticed and you didn't tell her to back the hell up either!"

I was in no mood to be romantic anymore, so I walked off the dance floor in a huff and went upstairs to the private room Reggie had reserved for all of us. I was all out of breath by the time I stormed into the black and gold room, the room where Reggie and I first met. I poured myself a cup of 7up and sherbet punch and sat down at one of the decorated tables.

Reggie walked in and sat down beside me.

"Karena, why do you think I'd want that girl when I've got you?"

"Why were you lettin' her feel you up?"

"I can't help it if I'm irresistible to women." He joked.

I didn't want to but I ended up giggling anyway. I hated when I wanted to have an attitude then somebody came along and made me laugh! Sometimes a girl just wanted to be mad.

"Just tell me one thing: Is that the girl who called you the other night? I'm sorry, I meant the other morning?"

"No, that was not her. Kima doesn't have my home number. And by the way, the only reason why I lowered my voice is because I didn't want you to hear me goin' off on old girl."

I wanted to believe him, but this was not the first time I had noticed some weird behavior, regardless as to what Reggie's excuses were. I did not like feeling like he was hiding something from me and I started to think that maybe hooking up with him so quickly wasn't a good idea.

I'm sure that Reggie could see the doubt in my eyes. Man, it was like he knew me so well already. All of a sudden, Kima came bursting through the door.

"Well, there you are Mr. Compton number two," She said. "I was wondering if we could dance together, if you're *girl* wouldn't mind sparing you for a moment, of course."

Somebody turned the fire back up! I did not like the way Miss Thang said "girl", like I was some immature youngin!

"You know Kima; you kinda caught me at the wrong time. See me and Karena…"

I cut him off.

"Reggie it's cool. You two go ahead and dance and I'll meet up with you when the D J plays our song." I licked his lips while staring a dagger through Kima. She rolled her eyes and turned her head away.

I had no idea what *our song* was going to be and neither did Reggie, but I couldn't think of anything else to say without putting some base in my voice and adding a curse word or two.

"You do that," Kima retorted.

Before Reggie could protest, she grabbed his arm and pulled him out of the room. I gulped down the rest of my punch and sat there, trying to think of a song that would explain my feelings for Reggie and put Kima in her place.

Ty came bouncing in the door and plopped himself down into a chair. He was sweating and his shirt was halfway unbuttoned.

"Whew, I'm tired as hell and it's getting pretty toasty down there!" He gulped down a cup of punch.

"Yo, who is that broad Reggie's dancing with?" Ty asked.

"That's Kima, some tramp who works here."

"And you're letting a girl like that go off with your man? She seems like she's tryin' to take your place home girl."

"Damn that, she knows Reggie is mine. I just gave her permission to dance with him, but trust me he don't want her. I'm not pressed."

"I hear you. She ain't his type anyway, not if he's got a woman like you in his corner."

I smiled at Ty. He was so sweet and I really needed a pick me up.

"Thanks Ty that was a nice thing to say! So, where's Niya? I haven't seen my girl for a minute."

Ty shrugged his shoulders. "I don't know. She wanted to drink and I wanted to dance, so she had a little temper tantrum and stomped off to the bar without me. I've decided that I'm not gonna let her fuck up my night! This is the most fun I've had in a long time, so if she has an attitude, its best that she stay's outta my face."

"Well, it's a good thing that she didn't see you all hugged up with that girl you were dancing with. What's the 411 on her?" I asked him.

"Her name is Pam and she's a student at Clark-Atlanta, pre-med if I'm not mistaking." Ty was blushing and grinning like a boy with his first crush.

"Okay, giving Niya a run for her money! I hear ya!"

"It's not that. You may as well know that I've decided to leave Niya alone once we get back home. She doesn't want me and she shows me all the time through her actions."

"I'm sorry Ty. Niya doesn't know a good thing when it's staring her right in her face."

"What do you have to be sorry about? She has a mind of her own."

I was proud that Ty wised up and was going to leave Niya to her own vices. She tried to pretend like she didn't like him as much as he liked her, but let him decide to sample the juices of another's fruit and she'll probably hit the roof!

"Look, let's get back down there and dance! I think you've rested enough," I said. I took his arm and we headed back to the party.

Just as I thought, that Kima chick was on the dance floor shakin' her stank ass all over Reggie. She was flippin' her weave back and forth so hard I thought she was going to break her damn neck!

Reggie was behind her pretending to smack her ass. I started boiling all over again, but then the music slowed to a nice groove so that stopped all the booty shakin'. Kima tried to pull Reggie close but he backed up and begin looking around.

"Go get ya man, Karena!" Ty said and gently pushed me over towards the dance floor. He saw his college honey waving at him and went to dance with her as I made my way to Reggie.

I stopped dead in my tracks and focused on the song that was being played. It was "Always" by the group Atlantic Starr. At that moment, I knew that was our song.

"Mind if I cut in?" I asked. "Come on baby, this is our song."

Kima stepped back in surprise as we left her alone in the middle of the crowded coupled floor. I lovingly place my arms around Reggie's neck and we kissed passionately.

"I think this *is* our song," He said confidently.

Together, we rang in the New Year holding each other, tipsy as hell!

Reggie

I was sitting outside my Uncle Red's corner

store shooting the breeze with a few of my peeps,

Erick, Reece, and Mel. My uncle had one of the

first stores in the neighborhood and had been

notorious for feigning off potential robbers with his

trusty, semi-automatic rifle. Nowadays, nobody

tried to fuck with him and he was well respected

throughout the community.

The wind was whipping against my navy

blue jogging suit as I pressed my back to it. It was

kinda chilly outside and the would-be fresh air was

outweighed by the thick smell of cigar smoke.

A little boy came up to us and tried to push

us some over-priced candy bars, but Mel scared the

shorty so bad that he took off running, leaving the

candy behind. We all cracked up laughing.

"Hey little homie, you forgot your candy bars!" Reece hollered after him, but the boy was not turning back.

"Why would we wanna buy a candy bar from him for a damn dollar?" Mel asked. "We're standin' right outside the fuckin' store where we can get one for half that price!"

"You didn't have to be so hard on the little dude, Mel," I said. "He was just trying to get up on his hustle."

I heard a sound system booming down Ponce de Leon that seemed to have the earth shaking.

"Ya'll know that's Buster's big ass on his way down here!" Erick said.

The volume of the bass and the vibration in the cement increased as my cousin Buster pulled up to the curb in his white Navigator.

"What's goin' down cuz?" Buster asked as he stepped out of the truck.

He snapped his fingers at Shayna, one of his ladies, who was in the driver's seat and she quickly jumped out and headed into the store. I gave my cousin some dap and he offered to let me hit the blunt he was smoking.

"Nah, I'm cool," I said backing up.

"Aw come on man! This is that killa shit, no doubt!" Buster said.

"I'm on parole man! My P O got me pissin' every time I walk up in that piece. Besides, I promised my woman I'd try to quit smokin' all together."

Buster blew some smoke in my face and laughed. He was a big dude: tall and fat with a big Santa belly that wiggled when he laughed.

"Man please, who you tryin' to fool? You know you can't give up the Chronic! Karena got you in check like that?"

My cell phone rang and I noticed Kima's number. I swear that girl had been calling me ever since the New Year's Eve party. She knew Karena and I were together, but she didn't give a fuck. I could've killed Buster's ass for giving that girl my number!

"Look, there she go right now calling to check up on you," Buster choked out.

I was getting a contact buzz from his weed, so I sat down at the opposite end of the bench wooden bench that was outside the door.

"No, that wasn't her; it was Kima! She wouldn't even have my number if it weren't for your ignorant ass! You know who I'm holdin' it down with," I shot at him.

"You know Kima telling everyone on the block that it won't be long before she gets you, Reg!" Mel let me know.

"Look, my bad cuz," Buster said. "I guess I didn't really believe that you were ready for the one-woman type of thing."

"I'm not you, Buster!"

"Ouch! I said my bad, damn!"

"She probably just wants to suck your dick," Reece chimed in. "I say let her have at it, bro."

"I don't need her, I've got Karena and her skills are truly supreme! Fuck Kima!"

Buster yelled in the store at Shayna, "What's takin' yo ass so long to get me some chips and some damn Laffy Taffies? I got somewhere to go!"

"Where are you off to, B?" Erick asked.

Shayna hurriedly came out of the store and leaped into the truck, clutching the bag of goodies as if her life depended on it. Buster got back in his ride and it shifted under his weight. He checked his platinum Movado watch for the time and said, "Gotta go make this money!"

I had planned to surprise Karena at work and take her to lunch. Yeah, I was spontaneous and romantic like that! It was my day off so I figured I could hang out with her for a while then hit the crib for some much-needed sleep.

After I left the fellas, I headed over to J.R.'s Financial, the firm where Karena worked for her cousins. I stood outside and watched my baby through the glass window. There were about five people in the waiting area, reading over documents and other money-matter material. A delivery man who was clearly impatient and waiting to gain Karena's attention, which had been derailed to a phone call, was tapping his foot on the side of the large marble desk where she sat. She put the phone down and said something to the man. He stopped knocking his foot and stood up straight, Karena went back to her phone call and I walked in.

"Yes ma'am, that is correct," She said in a professional manner. "If you'd like, you could come in and talk to one of our highly qualified consultants. I'm sure they can assist you."

She looked up and winked at me while she scribbled something down on a post-it note. In the same manner, she signed whatever document the deliveryman needed and sent him on his way.

"Reggie, what are you doing here baby?" She asked, hanging up from her call.

"I came to see how your day was going and to take you out to lunch."

Karena smiled sweetly and gave me a quick peck on the lips.

"My day is a little hectic right now, but it's cool. And about lunch, I'm afraid I'm gonna have to take a rain check; I have a load of filing to do and a staff meeting in about an hour."

"Oh well, that's okay. I'm sure we can hook up later or something since it's my day off. I was hangin' out with my boys earlier so now I'm 'bout to go home and hit the hay; I'm tired as hell."

Karena rubbed the top of my head.

"I'm sorry about lunch, but we can do it another day. Thanks for the thought though."

I told her to have a good rest of the day and to say "Wassup" to Juan and Ryan. When I got home, I tried to go to sleep but I couldn't drift off so I called Buster to see where he was.

"Who dis?" Buster answered.

"Yo B, its Reggie. What are you doin' right now?"

A half an hour later Buster and I were sitting at a table in Mitzie's Café, a small soul food joint in Midtown, grubbin' on some homemade loaded potato skins and hot wings. I must have been craving them or something because those were the best wings and skins I'd had in a long time!

Our server brought us two Bud Lights and another basket of wings. Buster had sauce dripping from his mouth and I was sucking the skin off my fingers trying to get the last little bit of sauce off mine.

"So, Karena couldn't eat with you and I was your back up date?" Buster joked while smacking.

"Very funny, but she had a lot of work and a meeting so…"

"It's cool; I was hungry as hell anyway. Now I gotta go drain the dragon!"

He jumped up from the table and headed towards the back of the café. I felt like my stomach was gonna bust open; I was stuffed! I wiped the excess sauce from my mouth and cleaned my hands with one of the little moist cloths that were lying in a small silver case next to the condiments.

The news was on and I was concentrating on a story about some new building that was going to

be dedicated in College Park. Buster came back to
the table and sat down, breathing a sigh of relief.

"Damn, that felt good! Say Reggie, I
thought you said Karena had a lot of work to do?
Had a meeting or something?"

"She does, that's why you're here."

"Then how come you aren't back *there*?" He
said, pointing towards the back booths. "That's
Karena sitting back there ain't it, the last booth?"

I quickly turned around to see that he was
right; Karena was at the very last booth sitting close
to some stuffy-looking guy in a suit. He was
holding her hand and fingering the three-hundred
dollar diamond tennis bracelet I had given her for
our six-month anniversary. Any closer and the
dude would've been sitting on her damn lap! I

jumped up and was headed back there when Buster pulled me back down.

"Come on man, don't make a scene!"

"How are you of all people gonna tell me not to make a scene? My girl is up in here all goody-goody with some other nigga!"

"I know cuz, and I'm sure you wanna go clock that mothafucka she's with, too! I know the people who run this place and they're decent folks. We can't bust heads in here!"

I tried to calm down but I was mad as hell! *A lot of work to do, my ass!*

"Let's go, fuck this shit!" I said. I placed a twenty-dollar bill on the table and walked out the door.

Kima

"This weave is coming out today and I'm gettin' some micro braids," I told my girl, Shay. I ran my slender fingers through my tangled maroon tracks. We were sittin' up at her man's crib watching Jerry Springer reruns.

"Who's gonna do 'em for you?" Shay asked. She was braiding our other girl Candy's hair in zigzag corn rolls.

Shay could really braid some hair, but she didn't do micros because it took her a hundred years to finish and she has kids; those little bastards drove everybody so crazy that nobody wanted to stay at her house for too long! Besides, I wanted one of those African chicks to hook me up so that my shit would stay in for a while and I wouldn't have to be bothered.

"I'll get that girl Fatima who has that shop on Peachtree to do it," I said confidently.

"Damn, that girl is expensive!" Candy said. "Your job pays you enough for all that?"

Shay pushed Candy's head down so she could get a better hold on her hair. Her silver bracelets banged together as she continued to braid.

"My job is cool, but I don't make all that! I got some money coming in though."

"Where do you have money coming from? It's not from any illegal activity is it?" Shay asked in a worried voice.

That girl was always jumping to conclusions!

"Hell naw, I don't get down like that! Let's just say that I'm doin' a little moonlighting, that's all."

"What the hell is 'moonlighting'?" Candy asked.

"It's like working another job on the side. A part-time thing," I informed her.

We were still cleaning up the restaurant from the big New Year's Eve blast and I was beyond tired! I had sweated out my perm from all that damn dancing, and at some point, I had managed to break two nails, so my attitude was not the greatest.

"Kima someone's on the phone for you!" My co-worker Anna shouted.

"Great," I muttered under my breath. It had to be a bill collector because none of my people called me on the job; they all hit me on my cell. The year just got started and I was already being hounded by the money-sucking vampires!

"Hello, Kima speaking," I said into the receiver.

No one said a word.

"Hello? I said this is Kima speaking!"

I was just about to hang up when someone finally spoke.

"Hi Ms. Brown, you don't know me but I have a financial opportunity for you," The voice said. I couldn't tell if it was a man or a woman and I didn't wanna embarrass myself by assuming.

"Who is this?"

"My name is not important right now; the opportunity I have for you is, though."

I was beginning to get impatient.

"Look, I don't have time for games!" I stated. "I'm having a lousy day and as you know I already have a job. So cut the bullshit and tell me who this is, or you can talk to Mr. Dial Tone!"

"Okay, my name is Chi Chi."

"Okay Chi Chi. I know I don't know you, so where do you know me from?"

"If you agree to meet up with me I'll answer all of your questions and explain the proposition I have for you. Don't worry; I'm not a crazy nut, stalker, or any other weirdo. I'm just in a position to help someone out who's willing to help me in return and I know you are the person for the job. So, what do you say? We can meet wherever you want, other than your current place of employment."

Normally I would have hung up the phone if someone I didn't know called me and on the job at that. There was something about this person's voice; it was calm and soothing, like the feeling you

get from a cough drop when your throat is killing
you. Also, I really needed some extra money!
Christmas had set me back from buying presents
and getting in on all those holiday sales. My bank
account's stomach was growling with hunger from
being so empty.

I wondered what kind of job it was and why
the person couldn't do it themselves. Was it illegal?
Was I gonna get caught? I was nervous and
intrigued at the same time. I figured what the hell?

"Chi Chi I can meet you in about an hour at
the Payless shoe store across from The
Underground."

I reminded myself to get a fresh razorblade
on the way, just in case.

Karena

"Reggie, what's going on? You've been acting funny ever since I got here," I whined.

We were sitting at the dining room table eating Chinese food; well I was eating my sesame chicken and Reggie was playing around in his shrimp fried rice. He had barely completed a whole sentence in the time that I'd been here and he pushed me off him every time I tried to get close.

"Nothing's wrong," he responded quietly.

I got frustrated. There was obviously something wrong, but he wouldn't tell me what it was. I hated when Reggie wouldn't confide in me. For three days he had been so distant and short with me; he seemed to be pushing me away and I was getting tired of it. In my opinion, it is the worst when someone you love is going through something and you not only can't help them, but you don't know what the problem is if you were able to.

"You've been sayin' that you were fine since Tuesday," I reminded him.

"Then maybe you should get the point!"

Oh, so now he was getting smart!

I pushed my chair away from the table and stuck my leftovers in the refrigerator. I wasn't in the mood to stay around and endure his attitude, so I started gathering up my stuff to leave.

"Where are you going?" He asked.

"I'm leaving, why should I stay? You obviously have something else on your mind that you don't deem necessary to share with me, so I'm out!"

He got up from the table and took my coat out of my hands. He looked pitiful; I could tell there was something on his mind, but for some reason he couldn't get it out.

"Reggie, talk to me," I begged.

I placed my belongings back where they were and sat down next to him on the couch.

"Are you cheating on me, Karena?" Reggie asked after a long pause.

I just sat there with this confused look on my face. How could he ask me that?

"Excuse me? Why would you think I was cheating on you?"

"Because I saw you; I saw you with some dude in a suit in Midtown, the day you were supposed to be too damn busy to be with me!" He said aggressively.

I sat back in the couch trying to remember what he was talking about. I laughed out loud and snapped my fingers.

"The day we were gonna have lunch! Reggie that was Curtis; he does some of the legal work for the firm."

"Yeah, he looked like he was workin' something, alright!"

"This is what happened: I was in the middle of filing when Juan asked me if I could skip the meeting and bring Curtis up to speed on what's been going on. He had been out of town, so…Anyway, when he got there we were gonna order in some lunch, but he said he was tired of being inside and that he missed the city, so we went out."

"And that's all that was, a lunch meeting? 'Cause dude looked like he was tryin' to get up on that thang if you ask me!"

"It was just a meeting, you know I love you! You know how I feel about cheating! If that's what's been on your mind lately you should've come to me. You could've come up to me in the restaurant; I would have set the record straight right then and there."

"Naw baby, I would've gone off on him! Buster was with me and he talked me into dealing with it later."

"Yeah, three whole days later, so next time just talk to me; don't shut me out!"

I can't believe he thought I was cheating on him! Truthfully, it made me feel good that he was a bit jealous. I hope him seeing me with another man made him realize how I felt when Kima was all over him at the party.

Curtis was a bit close while we were at lunch. He asked if he could take me out to dinner, but I told him about my relationship with Reggie. I was flattered and for a split second, I actually considered accepting his invitation. I know that was wrong; Reggie did treat me well and I knew he loved me. There was something in the back of my mind telling me that not everything was all good with us.

It wasn't just the past few days that I've felt at odds with Reggie; that feeling had been in the pit of my stomach for a while. Maybe it was just insecurity on my part, I don't know. I had to get to the heart of things, otherwise there was gonna be trouble in paradise.

The next few weeks kinda flew by in a blur. I was working full time at the firm and spending most of my free time with Reggie and my new friend, Tia who owned the coffee shop down the street.

Tia Taylor was mad cool and we click right from the start! I was really missing being at home with Niya and the rest of my girls, so I decided to drown my sorrows with a steaming cup of French vanilla cappuccino; it reminded me of being at home and hanging out with Niya at Cup O' Joe's.

When I walked into TT's Coffeshop, I thought to myself, *this is a cool place!* The furniture was dark green and burgundy, the big fluffy kind you could just sink in and really get relaxed. There was amazing photographs all over the walls of children playing, couples walking and holding hands, and friends enjoying one another's company. About five steps led to a higher level called "The Information Superhighway" because that's where the internet and computer access was. That whole space was carpeted and had just about every shade of blue splashed around. That was my favorite part of the place.

I made my way up the stairs and sat on one of the couches. A waiter came up to me and I placed my order, sat back, and closed my eyes, taking in the ambience and the mulberry-scented aroma therapy candles. I could've drifted off to sleep right then and there; I was just that comfortable!

"You look like you feelin' mighty good right about now, girlfriend."

I looked up and Tia was standing over me. Her closely cropped, honey brown-highlighted hair looked good, and complimented her dark-brown complexion. She had beautiful green eyes that sparkled as she smiled.

"I've never seen you in here before. I'm Tia Taylor and this is my place." Tia extended her hand.

"I'm Karena Murphy, nice to meet you. This is my first time here, I work just down the street at J.R.'s Financial Consulting Firm and I was cravin' a FVC like you wouldn't believe."

"Oh, so you're a cappuccino lover, huh? I knew it. So what do you do on your job?" Tia asked sitting down.

"I'm an office assistant; I fax, do some filing, a little word processing, the basics. I love your establishment and this room is off the hook!"

"Thanks, it was my parents' gift to me for my 25th birthday. I had always wanted my own business so we made a deal; I'd get my degree in business management and they'd invest in my first place. Here I am!"

Tia was a breath of fresh air! She was so vibrant and full of life. I know I sound like a damn shampoo commercial, but I really needed a sista friend at the moment.

Niya and I hadn't really talked much lately, but not because I didn't try. I called her almost every week, but she was never home. When she was there, we only talked for a few minutes before she rushed me off the line, and even then, she didn't seem very interested to hear from me. Hell, I talked to Ty more than I talked to her; he called me long distance from his own phone and she wouldn't even buy a damn calling card to call me!

After that day at the coffee shop, Tia and I were like two peas in a pod! We went shopping together, double dated with the men in our lives, we even had cramps at the same time! (You ladies know what I'm talkin' 'bout!). When it was that time of the month, we got together and pigged out on chocolate and ice cream and complained about everything and everyone who was getting on our nerves! It was the best! Her honesty and candor was just what the doctor prescribed.

Reggie

I hated springtime because all it ever did was rain! For five days in a row it rained continuously, all different kinds; big fat drops, hard and fast, light and drizzly, and even that misty type that was just enough to get on your damn nerves!

I was on my way to meet up with Karena, Tia, and her man Brian for our couple's night out. Every week we decided to do something different together like dinner and a movie, miniature golf or something like that. This week we were headed to the rink for the late night adult skate jam. I hadn't been skating in years and I was looking forward to it, even if I was probably gonna be busting my ass the whole time.

At first, it made me feel weird having these "couple's night" things: I had never done this before and where I come from you don't date someone, you just kick it! But being with Karena is when I felt the most comfortable, not to mention that Tia and her boyfriend were pretty cool; they both seemed to have a good head on their shoulders.

I was nervous when I first met them because Tia is twenty-five running her own business, and Brian is only twenty-eight, has two degrees, and he's an engineer at one of the top architectural firms in Atlanta.

Although I was holding things down at the restaurant and making good money, I still somehow seemed like I wasn't good enough for Karena or her friends. The money I made now was nowhere near what I used to bring in when I was in the streets.

I must admit; I'm a hustla and I felt like the streets were calling me. I as much as I missed my old life, I wasn't going back to prison for nobody! I also wasn't about to fuck up the most important thing in my life, my relationship with Karena.

As it turns out, Brian had been locked up at one time too.

"Yeah man, I did five years at Rogers, down near Savannah. I sold it all; crack, heroin, cocaine, and everything else," He admitted.

We were all at his crib: a laid out, two-story condo in the city. You could look at this brotha and tell he'd been inside; he had that prison build goin' on, like Suge Knight, and I think we all know he was familiar with the locked-up way of life.

"Don't feel bad about ya past, Reggie," Brian coaxed. "We all go through things, but the important thing is to turn it around and make the system work for you."

"Reggie, Brian went to school while he was there. He took a few aptitude tests and they found out that my baby was some kind of genius! He got his GED, then a degree in architectural engineering," Tia boasted.

Karena squeezed my hand and had this proud look on her face. She was happy to be with me, degree or no degree.

"Well Reggie knows how much potential he has. I'm proud of him for getting out and handling his business, legally if you know what I mean," Karena said.

We had been spending time with those two since that night, and I was more than cool with couple's night now.

Fuck!

I had walked right out the house and forgot to brush my teeth! My breath was burnin' sores on my damn gums; I needed some mints, some Listerine, some somethin'!

I was already on the 85, but I couldn't roll up in there and scorch the hair off my woman's eyebrows with this bad breath, so I pulled into the Seven Eleven off the interstate. I hated being late and thanks to this detour that's exactly what I was gonna be!

I made sure my black Acura sedan was locked up tight and pushed my way through the smeared and stained double-glass doors. I nodded to the cashier, an older man who was wearing a shirt that said, "You don't wanna fuck with me!" and he nodded back.

I was trying to make up my mind between
the peppermint Lifesavers and the spearmint Tic
Tacs when I felt someone grab me around the waist.

"Hey you, whatcha getting' into tonight?"
A female voice asked.

There was Kima.

I really didn't feel like being bothered with
her ass! Especially not now, I was late enough
already. I settled on the Lifesavers, paid for them
and quickly ripped the package open and stuck one
in my mouth. Ahhh!

"Kima, I can't talk right now. I'm late and I
needed to be where I was headed fifteen minutes
ago." I tried to leave but she spun me around and
kept a tight grip on my gray Polo fleece.

"I saw you when you came in and since you don't talk to me at work, I figured I'd come over and speak," she cooed.

"I'm mad busy when we're on the job, you know the deal."

"But I see you on your cell phone all the time, so you must not be too busy."

Kima was about to earn herself a hand-delivered invitation to kiss my ass!

"I'm only on the phone for minutes at a time and that's either to my mama or my girl."

"I thought I was your girl?" She said palming my shoulder blades.

"We are cool and everything, but that's different. I mean…no disrespect, but I gotta go. Tomorrow at work I'll be sure to holla at cha, okay?"

I didn't wait for her to answer. I got the hell out of dodge instead so I could hurry up and get to the rink.

"Shit, damn, mothafucka!" I cursed out loud.

My two passenger side tires were flat! I mean flat, like I-have-to-buy-two-new-tires flat! I flipped up my cell phone and tried to dial but my battery had died and I didn't have my car adapter with me. There went my phone!

I found some change in my pocket and went over to the payphone.

"Oh, what the hell is this?!"

No dial tone! I should've known; the phone was so corroded and after a closer look, I saw that it was hanging on for dear life up against the rusted pole.

Damn, it was ten-thirty and I should've *been* at the rink by now! I saw Kima and another girl walking out of the store towards her beat up Chevy Caprice.

"Hey Kima, hold up a sec!" I dashed over to them. "Hey, can I use your cell? My battery is dead and I got two flats."

She told her friend to wait for her in the car and we walked back over to mine.

"Well no wonder you have flat tires, you pulled into a parking space full of glass." Kima said.

I looked down at the glass and at my tires, imagining how much some new tires were gonna cost me.

"I would let you use my phone, but Candy's dumb ass just broke the antenna! Now I can't get a signal."

"Fuck. The payphone's broken too. Fuck!"

"Why don't you let me and Candy give you a ride to wherever you need to go?"

After what happened at the party, I wouldn't dare have Kima take me to the rink! If Karena saw me with her, all hell would break loose.

"Naw, that's okay. I'll just go inside and ask the owner if I could use his phone."

"You don't have to do that, and really it's no trouble," Kima assured.

I didn't have many options left, and the more I sat there, the later I was gonna be. Karena was probably damning me to hell by now! I reluctantly followed Kima to her car and got in the backseat.

Kima had the filthiest car I had ever been in! There were crumbs all over the floor; paper, candy wrappers, and even an empty forty ounce bottle! Her light blue seats were now dingy and blotched with stains and there were strands of hair, different colors, scattered on them.

Her hair is probably fallin' out from that damn weave! I thought to myself and had to stop myself from laughing out loud.

Kima was playing her bootlegged radio so loud that I thought I was going deaf. I hated it when people tried to front and act like they had a system when all they really had was a lot of bullshit treble!

Looking out of her grimy, fingerprinted windows, I noticed that we were no longer headed in the direction of the skating rink.

"Oh Kima, I forgot to tell you I was going to the rink in College Park. I hope that's not too out of the way for you," I said.

Kima and her friend looked at each other suspiciously.

"Um, that's cool because I was actually headed over to my peeps house in East Point, but I forgot something at my crib and it's kinda crucial that I have it. I don't live far from here, so it'll only take a second for me to run in and grab it," Kima said.

When we pulled up fifteen minutes later to a modest set of duplexes, Kima and Candy hopped out.

"Be right back!" She said and they disappeared into the house.

I could only imagine what Karena was thinking right now. She had to know that I wouldn't just back out at the last minute without telling her. I looked down at my watch. Time was ticking, what was taking Kima so long?

Suddenly, both the girls flew out of the door and back to the car.

"Reggie, can I talk to you for a minute?" Kima asked.

"Kima, what's the deal? I thought it wasn't gonna take you long? I really need to get to the rink," I let her know.

"I know and I'm sorry. But see, my girl has an emergency back at her crib and she doesn't have a car. I was gonna let her take my car so she can go see what's up. You can stay here 'til she gets back; you don't wanna be around all that drama, trust me!"

I didn't wanna be here either! Before I could protest any further, Candy jumped her little ass behind the wheel, yelled something about being right back, and screeched off. I couldn't believe this shit!

I slowly trudged up the steps to Kima's house. If only I had of brushed my damn teeth before I left none of this would be happening.

The good thing was that Kima's house was cleaner than her car, but not by much. She had a beat up leather couch and dirty carpeting. Of course, her entertainment system was tight; she had a nice CD stereo, a flat screen TV, DVD player, and about a hundred movies. Some black folks could have milk crates for furniture and wouldn't give a

fuck as long as they had a nice TV and stereo

system to keep them entertained.

"Make yourself at home, Reggie," Kima

said as she cleared an armful of papers from the

couch to make room for me.

"Kima, let me use your phone please," I

asked.

"I don't have one. I got behind in my credit

cards and I had to let something go. Since I had my

cell I figured I'd survive, but now I don't even have

that!"

I wanted to throw her across the room!

First, I had no cell phone and then no car. Now

Kima had no home phone! How in the hell was I

gonna get up outta here and down to the rink, before

the jam was over?

"Man, this is some bullshit! What about your neighbors: do you think they'd mind if I used their phone?"

"Well they probably wouldn't mind, if they were home." Kima sat down next to me. "Would it really be so terrible for you to just stay here and kick it with me until Candy gets back?"

"I'm not saying that, but Karena and I had plans with some friends of ours. She's got to be worried and wondering what's going on," I told her.

"I'll tell you what; I'll talk to her for you and let her know it was my fault because I did agree to give you a ride. That way she'll know you weren't out tryin' to play her or anything. In the meantime, just chill," she responded.

Kima pushed me back on the couch and flicked the TV on. What choice did I have, I was stranded. Another thing on my mind was how I was going to explain this to Karena. I didn't wanna lie to her, but the last thing I wanted her to know was that I was with Kima, much less at her damn house. It wasn't looking top good for the kid right now.

"Reggie why don't you take your fleece off, relax a bit? Do you want a drink?" Kima said walking into the kitchen.

"No I don't wanna drink! I don't wanna watch TV, and I for damn sho ain't takin' my fleece off! All I want right now is to get to a phone so I can have someone come get me and take me to be with my lady and our friends, that's all I want!" I snapped at her.

Kima put the cups she had in her hand down and looked at me pitifully. I felt bad for talking to her like that, but I was frustrated and she just wasn't helping.

"I'm sorry; I didn't mean to speak to you like that. I'm just a little upset right now. Go 'head and hook me up with a drink," I told her.

Her expression changed and she filled the cups with some Hennessy and coke.

"I noticed that this was your drink of choice," She said handing me the cup. "Let's make a toast. Here's to…your girlfriend's level of understanding."

I prayed it would be very high tonight and we tapped the drinks together.

Three hours and about five Hen and cokes later, I was tipsy and even more upset. It took everything in me not to go off on Kima and all her little antics. I realized she was trying to see if something was gonna go down between us, but the chances of that happening where slim to none.

Before I was even done with my drink, she was back in the kitchen getting the bottle to refresh my cup.

"Naw, I'm cool. One more drink and I'll be passed out in here," I mumbled.

"That's okay, you could go ahead a take a little nap if you want to," Kima said seductively. "Why don't you put your feet up and relax."

"Why don't you leave me the hell alone? Kima you're cool and everything, but I already got a woman." I informed her.

"I know; I'm just trying to be a good hostess."

She massaged my dick through my pants and I could feel myself getting hard.

"Reggie, don't fight me. I've wanted you for a long time now. Karena will never have to know, nobody would. I could be better to you then she is; you just gotta give me a chance."

She managed to unzip my pants and before I knew it, she was on her knees going to work on my dick.

Oh shit!

I couldn't even lie; that shit was feeling so good and between that and the alcohol, she was hard to resist. I wanted to push Kima off, but the more I resisted the harder she sucked. I rested my hand on the back of her head as she bobbed up and down.

I tried to tell myself, *Comp you already gotta woman! Think about Karena, she would never play you like this!*

. I needed some strength, some divine intervention. All of a sudden, Candy came storming through the door and tossed the car keys on the floor.

Thank you, Lord!

Kima looked up surprised and I took the opportunity to zip up and try to get the hell outta there. It was after two in the morning!

"Candy, what took you so long?" Kima asked through clinched teeth.

She timidly shrugged her shoulders; a look of panic was on her face.

"Well, it's about damn time! Kima, now you can take my ass home!" I yelled.

Well, I guess I won't be skating tonight. Karena was gonna be pissed! Kima looked like she was mad about something, probably the fact that

Candy blocked her flow. She didn't have any more excuses now; she had to take me home!

When sat in silence on the drive to my house. Kima seemed to be deep in thought; she had both hands on the steering wheel and sat up with her back straight, eyes planted forward. She not once looked over at me or anywhere else for that matter. I guess she told herself that she had had enough of my black ass for one night, especially since she was caught off guard with a dick in her mouth!

We pulled up to my apartment. I sat there for a while; Kima still didn't look my way. At first, I was going to thank her for the ride. After I thought about the events leading up to the ride, I said fuck it!

"Look Kima, I won't tell anyone about what went down back there at your crib, I promise." I told her before I got out.

"Yeah, me either. Peace."

I didn't even get a chance to shut the door all the way before she pulled off.

Karena

"Karena, girl you look awful!" Tia said

when I walked into the coffee shop.

I felt like hell; my head was aching, my back

was killing me, and I was very congested. I had a

sinus infection; got one twice a year and they

always hit me right in the ass!

"Well then my looks must match my

feelings 'cause that's exactly how I feel," I told her.

I almost crawled my way upstairs to The

Information Superhighway then collapsed in my

favorite spot on the long, light blue couch. My head

was spinning and thumping at the same time and I

wondered why I had dragged myself out of bed in

the first place.

As if she were reading my mind Tia asked, "Why did you drag yourself outta bed? You need to be at home poppin' pills and getting some rest."

"I need a cappuccino; the steam will help to open me up."

Tia shook her head in disbelief.

"No you didn't come all the way here for a damn cappuccino! You should have called me; I would've just brought you one. Come on, I'm driving you back home and I'll grab a cab back here."

She was right; I was really in no shape to be out of bed, much less driving. Tia helped me up and we walked back downstairs.

"Lemme just tell someone where I'm going. I'll be right back!"

Tia disappeared to the kitchen. I noticed Kima at the counter and prayed that she didn't notice me. I was in no mood for that girl. I sat down at one of the tables with my back to her, but it was too late; she wasted no time coming right over to me after she had paid for her coffee and muffin.

"Hey Karena," she said in a cheery voice. "You don't look so good, hon."

"How very observant of you," I said sarcastically, rolling my eyes.

"So, how was your little skating outing the other night?" Kima asked snidely. She pulled up a chair and made herself right at home. How did she know about that?

"How did you know I went skating?" I asked.

"Oh, Reggie didn't tell you? I ran into him at the store. He wasn't interested in going, so he kicked it at my crib. I thought you knew."

"Reggie would not have stood me up and our friends to go hang out with you! Now if you don't mind, I'm waiting for someone," I snapped.

"Karena, I'm sorry to bust your bubble, but he was with me the other night. Tell me something; what time did Reggie tell you he made it home that night?"

"That's none of your damn business!"

"Was it sometime after two, perhaps?"

Kima eyed me closely with a smirk. I sat there motionless, blinking in confusion. Reggie did get home after two because he had called me and begged me to come over. His version of what happened that evening was nowhere near close to what Kima's was.

Reggie told me that his car broke down and his cell phone died so he used the phone in the store to call and ask Spanky to come and get him. Spanky was busy with his girl at the time and he could not get in touch with anyone else, so he had to sit there and wait for him. He said he tried to call me a couple times, but my voicemail just kept coming on.

I knew Kima wanted Reggie; that was not a big secret. It wouldn't have surprised me one bit if she were lying just to try to get my feathers ruffled.

"If you're trying to get me to think that something went down between you and Reggie just forget it. If he wanted you, he wouldn't be with me.

I was the one who ended up at his house that night, not you!" I fired at her.

"True, but that was only *after* the fact. And if you don't believe that anything happened between us just take a look at this."

Kima took a DVD out of her backpack and slide it across the table to me. What kind of games was this girl playin', and where was Tia?

"Okay, sorry it took me so long. I had a small emergency!" Tia said as she came whizzing over to me. She stopped suddenly when she saw Kima and the smug look on her face. Tia looked Kima up and down and made a face like something was stinking.

"Well, look at the time!" Kima exclaimed as she got up. "I must be heading off to work. Oh and by the way Karena, Reggie may be with you now, but it won't be long before I'll have your man and you'll be single."

Tia looked at Kima like she wanted to slap the shit out of her as she made a quick exit. I picked up the DVD and held it tightly.

"What was that all about?" Tia asked.

"She claimed that Reggie was with her the night his tires were messed up; when we went to the skate jam. She told me to look at this if I thought she was lying."

"Karena, throw that shit in the trash! You know that bitch is after your man, she just wants to try and break you two up!"

I knew Tia was right. Even though he had explained the situation to me about what happened that night, my old insecurities came back to haunt me and I felt compelled to look at the video.

"I gotta look at this, T!" I said and we headed to the parking lot.

Thank God I had finally moved into my own apartment! I was grateful for the privacy, which was gonna really be needed if there was some incriminating evidence on the DVD against Reggie.

Tia thought she was slick: she tried to get me to go right to bed as soon as we walked into my one-bedroom flat, but I wasn't havin' it! I wanted to see that video and the sooner the better.

"Tia I'm not going to bed until I see what this is all about!" I told her.

She gave up trying to convince me otherwise and turned on the DVD player. It took me awhile to push the play button on the remote. Whatever was on this tape was gonna tell me one of two things: either my boyfriend really did love me, or he was a boldface liar! Tia and I both sat on the couch and watched in silence.

Oh my God!

There it was staring me right in my face; Kima was on her knees suckin' my man's dick! You should've seen the look on his face!

I continued to watch in horror: the camera seemed to focus in on Reggie as his eyes rolled up into the back of his head and his mouth swung open. His hand was on Kima's head, guiding it up and down. Moans, slurps and humming noises came from that whore as she sucked him off faster and faster. More moans. Cuss words. Kima's voice telling my man how she knew she could make him feel good.

I felt sick to my stomach! How could he play me like this? It took everything in me to admit my feelings to him and this is how he repays me, by letting some tramp go down on him. That dick was supposed to belong to me! Kima looked straight into the camera and winked before using a small remote to click it off.

"Oh girl, are you okay?" Tia asked solemnly. She held my hand and rubbed it softly. "I'm so sorry, Karena. I can't believe Reggie would do something like this!"

"That makes two of us," I said softly, never taking my eyes of the TV screen.

"Tia, do you think you could stay for just a little while longer?" I asked.

"Say no more! I'll go call my assistant manager."

Tia went to make her phone call. I turned the TV off and stretched out on the couch. This is why I never wanted to fall in love; you only ended up getting hurt! I thought finding Reggie was the best thing that ever happened to me and we had been so happy. Now my heart was breaking and the only man I ever loved had played me like a fucking piano!

Reggie

Karena sounded terrible when I called her from work, so I decided to take off early and surprise her with some homemade beef stew. I knew she liked my mom's recipe and they had plenty left over from dinner last night.

"Honey, I'm home," I joked as I let myself in.

We each had a key to each other's places and mine came in handy now; Karena really needed to stay in bed. To my surprise, Karena was fully dressed, up and at em. She was staring at the television with a blank look on her face. I walked over and kissed her on the forehead.

"Baby, you still have a fever. You should be lying down," I told her.

I went into the kitchen and begin heating up the stew. I filled Karena's favorite glass, the one that said "Ohio Style" with some pineapple juice and placed it on the counter.

"I've got something for you; beef stew. Mama told me to tell you to eat every bit of it, too."

"I've got something for you too, Reggie. Come sit next to me; this won't take long." Karena muttered.

Her throat must've still been sore because I could hardly hear a word she said. I joined her on the couch and handed her the juice.

"Here baby, this juice will help soothe your throat; you need to drink," I advised her.

"And you need to watch!" She grabbed the glass from my hand and turned on the TV.

"Oh fuck!" I heard myself say from the screen. There I was at Kima's house with her on her knees and in between my legs. Where did that come from? She recorded herself going down on me? That fuckin' bitch!

I must have been too fucked up from the Hennessy because I didn't remember all of that; pushin' her head down, moanin' and shit. It looked like I was enjoying her; like I really wanted her. My mouth was dry and all I could do was gulp. I blanked out for a minute; the last thing I saw was Kima winking into the camera.

I couldn't do or say anything, the proof was right there in my fuckin' face!

Karena calmly turned off the television and took a sip of her juice.

"Get the fuck out," She said in a quiet and polite voice.

"Baby, let me explain. It's not what you think…"

"Not what I think? Not what I think?! I think my man cheated on me! The proof is right there to back up what the hell I think!" Karena screamed.

"But it didn't exactly happen like that! I had a few Hennessy and cokes and she caught me off guard. I pushed her off me!"

"So, now you gonna blame it on the alcohol right? That's every cheater's damn excuse! 'It was dark, we were drinking!' Save that bullshit! And I saw you push her alright; you pushed her head up and down to please you, that's how you pushed her!"

Finally, it hit me; Kima had set me up!

Everything was too much of a fuckin'
coincidence; her running into me at the store, her
offering me a ride, and her friend's so-called
emergency that left me stranded at her crib. She
probably even slashed my tires and broke a bottle
near my ride to make it look like I rolled over the
glass! Gatdayum, that bitch was hustlin' *me* of all
people!

"Karena listen, Kima planned that shit! She
must have set up the camera while I was in the
bathroom or something! I swear I didn't willingly
do anything with her!"

"So I suppose she drugged you, too? Is that
what you're tryin' to tell me?"

My head was banging! I couldn't believe all
this!

"Reggie, please leave! Get out!"

Karena broke down. I had never seen her cry before, not even get teary-eyed. I knew she was hurt and I had no way of comforting her.

"Baby please don't do this," I begged.

"I said get the fuck out!"

I headed to the door, Karena right on my heels.

"Hey Reggie," she called. "The juice is supposed to soothe my throat, right? Will it soothe my heart as well? Huh?"

She pushed me out, threw the bracelet I'd given her at me, and slammed the door in my face.

Kima was gonna pay for this shit! Because of her, I may have just lost the love of my life!

Kima

"Look, I've done everything you told me to do, so where's my money?" I yelled into the phone.

This was the second time I was arguing with Chi Chi about my money being late. Reggie was fine as hell; don't get me wrong, but the point of all this shit had been strictly to earn a little extra cash.

Contrary to popular belief, I'm really a nice person. I wasn't the home wreaking type, but I was drawn into the situation by the cash reward that was provided. As much as I did want Reggie, I wouldn't have gone through all this trouble just to be spiteful. That wasn't my style. Heaven knows I didn't have to trick a man into being with me! All these games were purely because of my love for money! Shameful isn't it?

"I told you you'll get your money! Now there's just one more thing I'd like you to do," Chi Chi said.

"I'm not doin' a mothafuckin' thing until I get the money you owe me! After that, then we can talk about your next mission. By the way, it will be the last. I'm tired of this shit!"

"You seemed down for it when I first offered you the money!"

"Well, that was then. Reggie is cool people; he hired me when no one else would and his family has always treated me decently. I hate to admit it, but Karena hasn't done anything to me either and I know she and Reggie really love each other."

"Oh please; someone break out the violins!" Chi Chi mocked.

"Look, fuck you a'ight! You're the one who sought *me* out!"

"And you're the one who needs the money, right?"

Chi Chi had me there.

"Okay, okay. But can we hurry and wrap this shit up?"

"No problem; I think my mission will be accomplished very soon. Here's what I want you to do next..."

Reggie

It had been three weeks since Karena slammed the door in my face and I'd never been so damn miserable! Any other girl could have done the same shit and I wouldn't have given a fuck. Karena was my woman and it was tearing me up inside that she didn't want to have anything to do with me.

I was lounging around my parents' house watching ESPN with my Pops. He tried to make me laugh by cracking jokes on the different players but it wasn't working; I was in no mood for humor.

"Son, why don't you try calling Karena?" Pops suggested. He took a sip of his beer and bit into one of the monstrous turkey sandwiches he'd made for us.

"I've been callin' her every other day for three weeks! She won't return my calls. I've gone by her house, her job, and even Tia's coffee shop to try to explain, but she ain't tryin' to hear me," I said.

I had filled Pops in on all the gory details of that night. I also told him that Kima was behind the whole thing; she tried to sabotage my relationship with Karena and it worked!

"I just can't believe that Kima would do something that childish," Pops said.

"Well believe it! I should've known that whore was trouble. I want her ass fired; I don't want her working for us anymore!"

"Now Reggie I know you're angry with Kima, but we can't fire her."

"Why can't we fire her? She purposely meddled in my personal business and ruined everything. Get her the fuck outta there!"

"First of all: I can't fire Kima unless she did something to jeopardize the business or unless her work was unsatisfactory. Second: watch your mouth. Remember, I'm still your father," He instructed.

"I'm sorry; I didn't mean to be disrespectful. I just can't believe I have to go to work every day with someone who's made my life a living hell! What's really fucked…I mean messed up is that she doesn't even care! She's not even sorry about what she did!"

"Jealousy is a horrible thing, Reggie; it can turn you into a person you never thought you'd be.

Kima really likes you and seeing you with Karena
must have really got to her."

"Yeah, but she already knew that even
before I met Karena I wasn't tryin' to push up on
her."

"But maybe she thought that if she would
never have you she could find some sort of way to
get you and Karena to break up; that way you'd be
single and there'd be a sliver of hope for her."

Check my Pops out trying to sound all Dr.
Phil-ish on me. I didn't care what excuses he tried
to make for her, Kima was not gonna have the last
laugh this time.

Can you believe she tried to talk to me at
work like nothing happened? She walked right up
to me the same as she did every day. She even

acted like she wasn't the one who showed Karena the tape.

"I don't know what you're talkin' 'bout!" Kima insisted. "I never showed Karena the tape!"

I would've called her into my office (yeah a brotha got his own office!) but I wanted to make sure we were in public, so if I got the urge to bust her ass there would be people around, but not too many, to remind me to think twice.

"There shouldn't have been a gatdayum tape to begin with!" I hissed. "Why'd you set me up like that?"

"I wasn't trying to set you up. Listen; you know I'm feelin' you and everything, but I know you're with somebody. I just wanted to fulfill a fantasy that I've had about you since the moment we met. The tape was supposed to be for my personal enjoyment; it was never meant to break up you and Karena."

Kima was trying her best to convince me but I wasn't about to fall for the okeydoke, again. Some customers came in and we put on our best faces and turned on the professionalism.

"Welcome to Compton and Company," I said to the women.

"Enjoy your meals, ladies," Kima said sweetly, and we both flashed them smiles that should've earned us Academy Award nominations. As soon as they were out of sight, the smiles faded and it was game on!

"How did Karena get the fuckin' DVD?" I wanted to know.

"Candy must have taken it. She's been staying with me because she and her man fell out.

She got mad at me over some stupid shit and she knew about it, so she probably took it and gave it to Karena to get back at me. I swear Reggie, it wasn't me."

"I don't give a fuck what you say right now, Kima. Just remember this; you need to stay the fuck up outta my business! Don't talk to me when you see me around, don't apologize to me, hell don't even fuckin' think about me no more! I knew you were a trick ass bitch from the jump!"

I thought Kima was gonna break down right there in front of the bar. Her bottom lip quivered and her eyes filled with water. She was always trying to play the tough roll like she had everything under control. She was cracking right in front of my face, clearly devastated by the things I'd said to her and I didn't give a fuck!

"I'm not feelin' so good all of a sudden,"
Kima whispered. "I think I'll take off work early if
that's all right."

"I don't care what you do, Kima."

She slowly removed her apron and went to
the back to get her stuff. As she was walking out
the door, my mom came up to me and asked,
"Where's Kima going?"

"She's sick, needed to go home," I told her.

She's sick alright; in the damn head!

"I saw you two talking. You guys looked
pretty intense; is everything alright?" Mom asked.

"Not by a long shot! Look, I'll go help out
her table."

I left my mom with a questioning look on
her face. I didn't have time to give her all the

details. I had to concentrate on getting my woman back!

It was after midnight by the time I was able to head home. My body ached; I was stressed. Why was I letting Karena get to me like this? She didn't wanna listen to me so I should've said to hell with her and went on about my business. I guess you can't just right someone off that easily if you claim to love them.

I saw the police lights flashing, signaling me to pull over. I knew I wasn't speeding; then again, my mind wasn't exactly on my speed at the moment. I was too deep in thought about the mess I was in with Karena.

I pulled over and took out my license. I made sure to turn my music down low, I didn't need any extra fines added to the ticket I assumed I was about to get. The officer tapped on my window.

"Reginald Compton?" He asked.

Nobody had called me Reginald in forever and I was rather taken by surprise.

"Um, yes sir. How fast was I going, Officer?"

"This isn't about your speed, young man. Would you step outta the car please?"

This shit was not good. I started getting flashbacks from the last time I'd been pulled over; the time I was arrested and my ass was sent to prison for three years! I got out of the car as I was instructed.

"Officer what's this all about?"

"We received an anonymous phone call that this vehicle has allegedly been involved in narcotic sales and distribution."

I was beyond shocked!

"I haven't been selling drugs to nobody! You've been misinformed, Sir." I told him.

"Step out of the car, please!" Officer whoever was getting a little testy.

"Look, I don't sell drugs! I'm the manager of Compton and Company restaurant downtown. I just got off work."

"This will only take a second, I'll need to search the vehicle," He informed me. Another officer exited the cruiser and joined him in his search.

This was fuckin' incredible! I was standing on the side of the fuckin' freeway, the 20 to be exact and it had mad traffic on it, too much for it to be the hour it was. It was clear that people were trying to see what was going on; nobody drove less than fifty miles an hour on the freeway in this city unless they were trying to be nosey, regardless of what the speed limit sign read.

"Jones, I think we got somethin' over here," the officer said.

I wanted to know what it was he thought he found in my ride. I eased back over and saw him pulling out a baggy full of little vials; cocaine vials.

"Oh hell naw, that shit ain't mine!" I yelled.

"Let's go *homeboy*; you're under arrest!"

They handcuffed me tightly and eased me into the backseat of the police car.

I know I was on the straight and narrow and hadn't been around any drugs! Somebody put that shit in my ride, but I had my car locked up tight.

Who could've gotten inside?

I knew Kima's ass wouldn't be stupid enough to try to pull another stunt, not the way I lit into her ass! Besides, she ain't smart enough for this shit; whoever did this knew all about the game of gaming.

I pressed my throbbing head up against the cool window as we headed to the Dekalb County police station. I was being set up again, but this time the stakes were much higher.

Somebody was trying to get me sent back to prison.

Karena

I peeked out from under the covers just enough to read the time on my alarm clock; 3:23 in the damn morning and someone was callin' me!

My phone had been ringing off the hook for the last fifteen minutes and I had desperately tried to ignore it. Juan needed me to come in to work a little earlier because of an emergency meeting; I needed all the sleep I could get!

My whole body had been submerged under my satin comforter, so I just let my arm out enough to answer the phone that was on my nightstand.

"Hello?" I answered in a deep, groggy voice.

"Karena, this is Janine. I'm sorry I woke you up," she said.

"Mrs. Compton, is everything alright?" Reggie's mom sounded frightened.

"No, Reggie got arrested! They're holding him at Dekalb County Jail," she said.

I threw the covers off me and sat up on the side of the bed.

"Arrested for what?" I asked.

"Possession of cocaine; they pulled him over and found it under his car seat! They said they got an anonymous tip so they tailed him. But Karena, we both know that Reggie hasn't been selling drugs!"

I didn't say a word; there was nothing I could say. I didn't want to believe that Reggie had started selling drugs again; there was really no need for him to go back to that. After what happened with Kima, I didn't know what to believe about the boy! I was still hurting from that; this was the last thing I needed.

"Karena, I know you and Reggie aren't on the best terms right now, but I wanted you to know what was going on. He tried to call you himself but you wouldn't answer the phone," Janine said.

"I didn't answer the phone because I have to get up early. Mrs. Compton, I'm sorry Reggie is in this predicament, but there's really nothing I can do for him. Take care." I hung up the phone.

I did love Reggie and I hoped that they'd let him go, that everything would be okay. I just couldn't allow myself to get involved.

Why should I care after the way he played me? Him being with Kima wasn't the first time either; the times some girl, whom I'd never met, kept calling in the middle of the night and the way he acted with Kima at the New Year's Eve party all contributed to my crushed feelings.

I thought I had let all that shit go. Reggie and I were doing so well, our relationship was strong. He just had to let that heifer suck his dick and fuck our good thing up!

I felt my walls building back up; the ones I had knocked down just for him to be able to enter into my life. It took a long time for me to be able to do that and this was the thanks I got: a cheating boyfriend.

Love or no love: I was not about to let Reggie make a fool of me twice.

Reggie

Ain't this a bitch!

I was sitting in yet another darkened, lifeless interrogation room. I got a splinter in my hand from the old wooden chair they pushed me into and it was throbbin' like hell. A lone 1980's-looking tape recorder sat in the middle of the tilted gray table, awaiting the confession I was not going to give.

For three hours, they grilled me and asked me the same questions repeatedly: "Who sold you the coke?" "Who were you gonna sell the coke to?" "Son, why would you wanna go and mess up your parole?" "There was a lot of coke found in your car; you know you could get five years for this, easy?"

I tried to call Karena but she wouldn't answer. Figures, she was still pissed about the Kima

situation! I finally got in touch with my parents.
They called my lawyer, Sam Reiner and they were
on their way to get me.

Mr. Reiner and the officers that arrested me
stepped into the room.

"Let go Reggie, we're outta here!" Mr.
Reiner said.

He didn't have to say a word! I quickly got
up and followed him down the hall towards the
entrance. My parents were standing at the door; my
mother had a worried look on her face. When she
saw me, she grabbed and hugged me tightly.

"Baby, are you okay?" She asked.

"Yeah Mama I'm okay." I looked her in the
eye. "You know I didn't do it, don't you?"

"Of course we do, Reggie." Pops cut in.

"They didn't have enough to hold you on; too much circumstantial evidence. The lock on your passenger's side had been popped; anyone could've planted those drugs in your car. Plus, your whereabouts could be irretrievably proven, so they had to let you go," Mr. Reiner said.

Officer Jones shoved my belongings in my hand. I signed the release form and rolled out.

"Did anyone try to get a hold of Karena?" I asked while my parents drove me back to my place.

"I talked to her," Mom said quietly.

"I guess she didn't wanna hear it, huh?"

"She's just upset, baby. You guys were already going through some drama, and then I call her in the middle of the night and tell her that you've been arrested."

I know my mom was trying to console me but the shit wasn't working. I felt myself growing angry.

"She's upset?" I roared. "She's not the one who's gettin' set up! She's not the one who just got arrested for some bullshit!"

There was no point in trying to reason with me. My parents realized that and didn't continue to talk to me. I didn't say another word until they dropped me off.

"Now Son, don't go trying to play vigilante; hell bent on seeking revenge. That won't solve a thing and will most likely get you into further trouble. The cops are really gonna be watching you now and you're still on parole," Pops warned as I jumped out of his SUV.

He must have been reading my mind 'because that's exactly what I was thinking about. I knew he meant well, but damn all that! Somebody was gonna pay for fuckin' around with me!

To get them to leave I told him, "Pops, I hear you. I just wanna go inside and forget about this. I have a lot riding on my release and I will not mess that up."

"Are you givin' me your word on that?"

I crossed my fingers and silently asked God to forgive me for boldly lying to my father's face.

"My word is bond."

By the time summer officially came, rolling around I had said a big fat "fuck you" to Karena. I had called and called after my little stint at the police station; I had sent her flowers and cards to her job, just to see if she was alright. I had even gone to Tia to see if she could help a brotha get back in, but that was a lost cause; she still wanted nothing to do with me.

It was slave hot in the city! Every day the temperature started out at eighty degrees: we talkin' 'bout at eight in the morning! I would see all the construction workers, roofers, and everyone else that had to work outdoors on my way to work, roasting in the blazing sun. I thanked my lucky stars that I didn't have to do that shit!

And the ladies! The women said to hell with the long-sleeved shirts and slacks that had their skin bound because of the cool weather; woman had let their bodies out in those booty shorts and halter-tops. As far as the eye could see, tits and asses were everywhere!

It had been too long since me and Karena had had sex and since we were no longer together, I began to acquire another frame of mind; fuck relationships! I was gonna go out and find some broad to fuck into oblivion!

My cousin Buster and I were kickin' it at the 8 Ball Pool Hall. I was fucked up from drinking too much Tequila and kept missing the ball every time I tried to hit it with the stick.

"Man, you're drunk! Sit your ass down before you hurt somebody up in here!" Buster said.

"Dude I'm cool, I just need to focus my eyes," I told him.

After a couple blinks, I cleared my throat and broke the group of balls. Buster watched in amazement as I knocked every single ball into the pockets.

I stood up straight and calmly placed my stick on the table. I told Buster, "I'm sober enough to know that you owe my ass fifty dollars, mothafucka!"

"Whateva, man!"

Buster reached in his pocket and pulled out the cash. He got quiet as he began setting up the balls for the next showdown.

"Say man, I saw Karena the other day at the zoo; I had taken my little shorties there," he said.

I still thought about her all the time, but after the way she left me hanging I didn't wanna admit it to nobody!

"So?" I said smugly.

"Aw don't act like you don't give a shit! I know you still love that girl!"

"Was she with her fam?" I asked.

"See there; why you wanna know who she was with if you don't care?"

I shot Buster an evil look.

"Okay, okay. She was with that dude we saw her with at Mitzie's and this time I'm sure it had nothing to do with work."

"I knew that nigga wanted her! He must have been markin' his territory that day," I said angrily.

Buster laughed and said, "Yeah well you let her ass go, so don't hate on the brotha that snatched her up."

"Let her go my ass! She didn't want me no more!" I was getting heated.

"Uh huh, and what was it that brought her to that conclusion?"

I didn't even wanna go there. Buster knew about what went had gone down with Kima.

My stomach started growling so I walked up to the food counter. There was so much smoke in the place that I could hardly see where I was going. The girl working the counter had her back from me, so I couldn't see her face.

"Excuse me; I wanna place an order please."

My jaw dropped as the girl turned around; I was face to face with Kima. She had quit the restaurant after I cussed her ass out that day and I hadn't seen her since.

"Kima, I didn't know you worked here"

"Hey Reggie, what can I get for you?" She sounded too professional.

"Um, an order of cheese sticks and a Pepsi," I fumbled.

I had to admit: Kima was lookin' good. Her skin was smooth, her Baby Phat outfit tastefully hugged her curvy body, and that ridiculous weave she always wore had been traded in for braids. I started thinking about Karena and how her hair was always braided, so I turned my head.

Kima moved her way through the kitchen area and poured my drink.

"Here's your Pepsi and that'll be $4.50." She never looked directly at me.

I handed her the money. She hastily dropped it into the register. A bell chimed and she took my cheese stick out of the oven and handed them to me.

"Here you go, enjoy," she said, obviously trying to get rid of me.

"Hold up Kima! I think we should talk," I told her.

"Believe me; we talked enough the last time we were together."

I lowered my head and said, "I'm sorry about that day, I was just trippin'. How have you been? You quit the restaurant."

"Did you really think I was gonna stay after the way you treated me?" She asked. "I do have some pride, you know. Anyway, I've been cool, maintainin'; you know how it is."

"Yeah, I know. So what are you doin' when you get off work?"

"Why?"

"I thought maybe we could hang out; bury the hatchet if that's possible."

Kima shook her head and laughed.

"You think I don't know the deal?" She asked. "I know you and Karena aren't together anymore, so you must be lookin' for some rebound pussy."

"That's not what this is about."

"Come on now, I'm not stupid! Your hormones are probably ragin' and you need a quick nut!" She said harshly.

Damn, why did I even bother? See what happens when you try to be civil to somebody? I gave up, took my food and started to head back to Buster to finish our game when Kima called out to me.

"Reggie, I get off in an hour."

Kima

Oh God, if this is a dream please don't wake me!

When I got off work, Reggie and I drove out to a park not far from the pool hall. I cut off the lights and we jumped in the backseat.

We didn't even bother with any small talk and I could've cared less. Karena had let this fine man go and I was determined to put it on him so good that he would never think about her big ass again!

I tongued Reggie down forcefully. The thought of what was about to go down made me so wet and I couldn't wait for him to stick his dick inside me. He pulled my head back and began kissing my neck. That's my spot right there, boi!

I removed his shirt while he wriggled his way out of his pants. Damn he smelled so good! He didn't even bother unhooking my bra; he just pulled it up over my breasts and hungrily sucked me nipples.

"That feels good," I moaned.

I tore off my hip-hugging jeans and lacy thongs. This was no time to start beating around the bush! Speakin' of bushes, I was glad I had shaved mine this morning so Reggie wouldn't think I was hiding Buckwheat's twin between my thighs!

I knew how much Reggie enjoyed my last blowjob, so I maneuvered around until I could comfortably get my lips around his huge dick.

"Mmmm," Reggie moaned in pleasure.

I licked and sucked every inch of his dick until he was squirming all around. I let him finger me from behind as I continued to orally please him, only stopping a few times when a wave of ecstasy would take over.

"I want you to cum in my mouth!" I demanded.

I wanted to taste him, to swallow his salty spirits and let them rest in the pit of my stomach.

His hand was on my head; he grabbed a handful of my braids. His breathing quickened as he spoke: "You want it in your mouth, huh? Okay, here it comes! Oh fuck!"

I almost gagged as Reggie exploded and his sperm coated my mouth and throat. I had never been with a man who had so much cum! I swallowed every bit of it and continued to suck him off.

When I was sure he was finished I wiped my mouth and lay down on the seat with my legs opened wide. I thought he was gonna eat me out, but instead he covered his dick with a Trojan and plunged into me deeply.

"Oh yes, do it like that!" I screamed.

Reggie held both of my legs up to the ceiling and had me screaming like I was being murdered. His long, powerful strokes were just what I needed and I could no longer hold my climax at bay. After I hollered loud enough to shatter all the windows, I got on top and rode Reggie's ass into the sunset like he was a Clydesdale. For the next hour we sexed uncontrollably, rocking my car from side to side.

Damn Karena to the steaming hot pit of hell; this dick was finally mine!

Karena

As fall approached, I thought more and more about Reggie. Our one-year anniversary would have been this month and I was missing the hell outta him!

I tried to talk myself out of shutting him out; I knew I had fallen in love with him for a reason. My pride and my broken heart would not allow it.

I saw Reggie several times over the summer, but would never let him see me. No matter where it was I always managed to duck behind something so that I'd be out of sight.

Curtis Styles, the attorney from the firm, had asked me out one day when we ran into each other at Mickey D's. I was standing behind some lady with four spawns of Satan who all kept jumping up and down like some damn Jack in the boxes.

"I wanna happy meal!" One of them yelled.

"I do too." Another rang in.

"If ya'll don't settle down we're gonna leave and you won't get nothin'!" She warned.

That got the little hooligan's attention; each of them straightened up and kept their eyes on the prize: yummy, delicious happy meals!

I had been craving some nuggets and ate them just about every day. I'd just finished placing my order for some along with some French fries when I heard a deep voice asked me, "What kind of sauce do you like with your nuggets?"

I almost jumped out of my skin because I didn't know he was behind me. I slapped his arm and said, "Curtis you scared me to death!"

"I'm sorry, I just couldn't resist," he said chuckling. "Look, I've been meaning to ask you if you wanted to go out sometime. I know you were with someone, but I was hoping that you might be single now."

I really didn't want to date anyone; I still felt emotionally attached to Reggie. It had been over three months since I'd had a male companion sexually or otherwise. I really needed some attention and I enjoyed Curtis' company.

"I was with someone but that's over now, so why not?" I said.

"Have you ever been to the Atlanta zoo?" Curtis asked. "They have a huge reptile area and I remember you telling me once how you loved snakes."

"That sounds like fun; I'd love to go."

We went out several times after that. One time I had to cut an outing to a Saturday fun festival short because I got so sick and felt like I was about to pass out. Curtis thought it was from the heat and drove me back home. He was so sweet and although he understood that I still had feelings for Reggie, he made sure I knew that he was romantically interested in me.

"I'm sorry you got hurt, Karena," Curtis said to me one night over dinner at my house. "But if he was stupid enough to do something like that then you're better off without him. I just want you to know that I would love to get the chance to help you pick up the pieces."

I realized that the more I sat with him, the more I wanted to be with Reggie. As much as he had hurt me, there was still a lot of unfinished business between us. Before I moved forward, I needed to step back into the past and make things right with my first love.

"Curtis, I think you're wonderful. But I won't lie to you; I'm still in love with Reggie and I don't wanna play games and pretend that I'm not. We never officially ended things; we kinda just went our separate ways and there are a lot of loose ends that need to be tied before I can start something new."

"Well I won't tell you that I'm not disappointed, but I do understand. Maybe we'll get together in another life," Curtis said.

"Maybe we will."

By the time I showed Curtis out, I was clear on what I needed to do. I went over to the phone and just before I picked it up it rang.

Déjà vu.

"Hello?"

"Karena, it's me," Reggie said.

God, his voice was just as smooth as always!

"I know; I was just about to call you."

"Yeah right, sure you were. That was a joke by the way."

I smiled and I knew he was smiling too.

"Can we get together and talk?" He asked me.

"Sure, but not here and not at your house either."

"Let's get a room somewhere."

"It's not that kind of party! I just wanna talk."

"Don't get all feisty; I just wanna make sure we have some privacy that's all."

"Okay, meet me at the Motel 6 on Wesley Chapel in fifteen minutes."

The silence in the motel room was thick with tension. The curtains in the small, but quaint room had been drawn, overlapping each other to guarantee total privacy from the passersby outside.

It was weird being with Reggie after all this time. I kept my distance and sat behind the round table in front of the window while he leaned up against the drawers. His "Louisville" shirt and khakis looked good on him; everything he wore always looked good on him!

I wanted him to remember what he'd been missing, so I made sure I looked good enough to eat in my frayed jean skirt, brown V-neck sweater and brown ankle boots.

Reggie gave me a sorrowful look before clearing his throat.

"Look, baby I know things have really been a mess between us, but I wanna make them better."

"So just like that, you wanna get back together?" I asked him.

Reggie walked over to me and dropped to both knees.

"Well I don't expect it to be easy, but I'd like to try."

I didn't want to, but I couldn't help looking into those dark brown eyes of his. I used to love gazing into them, trying to figure out what was behind them; what they were trying to say when his mouth couldn't form the words. Plus, his long and full eyelashes made me absolutely weak!

"Karena," he whispered, "I love you to the third degree. I want you to be my wife, for me to be your husband. We've been through so much and it took me some time to get my head straight, but I'm in love with you; and I know you still love me!"

I couldn't stand it anymore. I got up and walked over to the bed. That was a big mistake! As soon as I sat down on the soft, king size bed, I began imaging us making love and how good it would feel. It would feel even better this time because my body was incredibly tense and nobody knew how to work it like Reggie: that I couldn't even lie about!

"I know that you love me and of course I still love you. But I haven't been feeling loved by you for quite some time now."

Now, I didn't look directly at him while I was talking, but I could feel his eyes practically burning a hole through my chest. I breathed heavily, not knowing what was going to come next. I closed my eyes and after what seemed like an eternity, I opened them realizing they were filling up with tears.

"So is this it for us, Karena? Are you officially letting me go? After all this time, you're giving up on me, on us?"

. Struggling, I managed to look at him. He looked so sincere and I wanted to forget this whole madness and run into his arms. I got all these flashbacks of our happy times, like the first time we met, and the first time we made love.

My doubts were still looming over me. I couldn't help but think about the tape of Kima going down on him and the fact that he had lied about being with her. I started tearing up.

"I just don't know how we could make our relationship work if we got back together. I'm at the end of my rope and I don't think I can hang on much longer," I sniffed.

"Then tell me what to do. I'll do whatever you want me to," Reggie pleaded.

I pondered his request then told him, "I want you to be honest. How long were you and Kima messing around? Tell me the truth or I'm outta here and we can forget the whole thing!"

Reggie's eyes sank and so did my heart.

"Okay, I fucked her. I swear it was after you and I had already stopped speakin' and it was only once. I didn't make love to her, go down on her, or treat her like I would've treated you. It was purely a physical thing."

Well, I wanted to know and I told him to be honest. *Suck it up, girl!* I told myself.

"Is there anything else?" I asked.

"No, I promise. What about you; I heard you were kickin' it with the lawyer-dude from your job, is that true?"

"We did go out a few times, but we never fucked if that's what you mean. I haven't been with anyone else. Curtis knew the deal."

"What deal was that?"

I looked deeply into his eyes.

"That I was still in love with you and that we had some things we still needed to discuss. I'm pregnant."

Reggie's eyes got wide.

"Pregnant? Are you sure?"

"I told you; I know my body. Plus, I went to the doctor and I'm about three months or so."

"Where you ever gonna tell me?"

"I would've gotten around to it, but we weren't talkin' and…I don't know why I waited so long. But baby or no baby I do know one thing: Reggie, I wanna try and work it out."

"I'll never hurt you again, Karena!"

We embraced tightly and vowed to make things work.

Kima

"Reggie, what are you doing here?" I asked giving him a hug.

I was lookin' a hot mess! I had just gotten out of the shower and had on some old cutoff shorts and a wrinkled flannel shirt. My American flag scarf had my braids covered and I know my breath was on fire because I stuffed a handful of salt and vinegar chips in my mouth on the way to the door.

"I'm sorry for not calling first, but I wanted to talk to you. Can I come in?" He asked.

"Sure. You'll have to excuse the way I look, I was just chillin'."

"It's no problem; I won't be here long."

I didn't like the sound of that. I also didn't like the sad look on his face. Sad faces meant bad news, and if it was coming from Reggie then I knew it was something that I didn't want to hear; he and Karena had gotten back together.

I tried to think positive; Karena had left my dude hangin' when he needed her the most. When he was arrested, she wasn't there. She never returned his calls, and she was dating someone else. I realized I had nothing to worry about and that Reggie was probably here to tell me he wanted to be with me on a monogamous level.

We sat down on my couch, in the very same spot where I got my first sample of him.

"I've missed you, Reggie," I told him. "I was wondering when you'd come over here and break me off."

I tried to kiss his neck but he pushed me away.

"I'm not here to break you off Kima. I'm just here to tell you something."

Please don't let it be what I think it is!

He continued: "Karena and I are back together; we're gonna have a baby and we've decided to work things out. I wanted you to hear it from me 'because you know how things are in the street; this way there is no he say/she say bullshit."

Karena was pregnant? My face was getting hot. Why couldn't he leave that bitch alone? I mean, I really didn't want to break them up, but it happened anyway. Now that I was close to getting him, they had to go and work shit out! Why couldn't he realize that I was better for him than she was?

"So you're gettin' back with her just because she's pregnant right, to make sure that the baby has both parents?" I hoped.

"No, that's not it. I love her, regardless of us expecting a baby"

"Reggie I don't understand; I thought you said she wasn't there for you? She left you hangin' when you needed her the most. I'm here and I would've never done that to you!"

I was on the verge of tears, but I couldn't let him seem me cry. I got up, went to the kitchen and poured myself a shot of Hennessy. I downed it and poured myself another. Reggie took the glass out of my hand.

"You don't need to drink, Kima. I don't mean to hurt you; I'm just tryin' to keep it real."

I looked at him and saw true sincerity in his eyes, a look that I'd never seen so effortlessly in anyone else I've ever known. I imagined that to be the look he gave Karena the first time he told her he loved her or the first time they made love. He must've given that look when they decided to work things out.

At that time, it became clear to me that I would never get him to look at me in that way. He was really in love and it was not with me.

"Thank you for being honest with me," I told him. "It's funny; I thought you were here to tell me that you wanted to be with me."

"I never meant to lead you on, Kima. Oh, and about that night at the park…"

I held up my hand.

"I already know; I *was* a rebound fuck. I knew that all along. I knew that was gonna happen as soon as you wanted to keep talkin' to me at the counter."

"Then why…"

"Why do you think? I knew that would've been my only chance with you so I took it."

He smiled at me and all the hurtful things he'd said to me and the horrible way I had acted didn't matter anymore.

"I know friendship is a long shot, but do you think we can call a truce for the time being?" Reggie asked extending his fist for some dap.

I knew there was only one thing that would make that possible.

"Well before I pound the rock, there are some things I should tell you that may make you change your mind…"

Karena

I took a whiff of the coral roses Reggie had delivered to my job. They were in full bloom and really stood out on my desk; I had been getting compliments on them all morning.

"So, things must be getting back on track huh?" Ryan said as she walked by.

"We're not all the way there but we are making progress. Reggie really is trying hard, we both are. I missed my man, girl," I told her.

I went to the coffee maker and poured Ryan a cup. She took a quick sip then placed it down and thumbed through a stack of files I had just pulled.

"Is he excited about the baby?" She asked.

"He's ecstatic and girl, if he calls to ask me how I'm feelin' one more time..."

"Well you gotta expect that. So, today's the day that I finally get the Crane account," Ryan said. "I've been working on this since the end of spring. Remember when I first met with that couple?"

"Were they the one's you took to that place in Alpharetta?"

"No, that was the Cooks. I took the Cranes to The Underground; they had never been before. That was the same day I saw your friend, what's her name, Yaniya."

I was in the middle of typing up a memo and stopped suddenly.

"You mean Yaniya? You saw her here in Atlanta? Are you sure?"

"Yaniya, that's it! Yeah, I'm sure; I saw her heading into Payless. I called her name but I don't think she remembered me 'cause she looked at me like I was crazy and took off. Speaking of taking off, I gotta get outta here! Wish me luck!"

Ryan grabbed her briefcase and left. I picked up the phone and quickly dialed Niya's number. She came to the city and didn't tell me, didn't even call me when she got here? I wondered what the point of her visit was then; she didn't know anyone else here but me.

"The number you're trying to reach has been disconnected..." a recording announced.

Niya's phone was disconnected? That couldn't be, not as much as that girl talked on the phone! I redialed the number but got the same message: "The number you're trying to reach has been disconnected. No further information..." I hung up.

What the hell was going on here?

I saw Reggie's car in the parking lot outside my apartment. I walked in and threw my coat and bag by the door. I wanted to hurry up a call home; somebody had to know how to get in touch with Niya.

"Reggie you won't believe what Ryan told me today at work!" I started.

My sentence came to an abrupt halt when I saw Reggie and Kima sitting at the kitchen table. Oh no he didn't; he had that bitch sitting up in my fuckin' house?!

"What the hell…" I was about to go off.

"Calm down baby, this time it's really *not* what you think," Reggie said.

I looked at them uneasily and Kima said, "Seriously Karena, I'm not here to cause any trouble. But there's something you need to hear."

She pulled out a mini digital recorder. Oh hell, the last time she had something to do with recording I got an eyeful of her sucking Reggie's dick!

"Just listen to this!" Kima said and pressed play

Karena

I finally got in touch with Niya, who had been staying at father's place. I thought that was strange because she always badmouthed him and talked about how much she hated him. She told me he was sick and they had made amends because he wanted her to come and take care of him for a while.

"Girl I was worried about you," I told her. "You hadn't called me or nothin'; it's been forever since we've talked!"

"Yeah I know. So what's goin' on down there? Are you and Reggie still broken up?" Niya asked.

"Girl, I don't know about him. He says he loves me but I just don't know."

"Maybe you should move back home, K. I mean, you don't seem too happy down there."

"I'd be a lot happier if my best friend would come down for a visit. Niya you haven't been here since New Year's!"

"That's right; it has been a long time," Niya said strangely. "I'll tell you what; I can get a bus ticket and be there this weekend."

"I'll be sure to pick you up."

Reggie

This was going to be interesting; Yaniya
was coming to town and she had no idea that
Karena and I had made up. After Kima spilled the
beans on her, I convinced her to play the tape for
Karena.

Yaniya was good; she came up with one
helluva plan to break us up and had bribed Kima
into helping her pull it off. She saw Kima flirting
with me at the New Year's Eve party and sought her
out from there; she even talked her into dancing
with me all freaky deaky and shit.

She had planned everything: the whole
situation with my tires, Kima videotaping herself
giving me head and she had Kima hire a bum to
plant the drugs in my car! Luckily, Kima had taped

every one of their conversations and Karena was devastated when she listened to it.

I felt so bad for my baby; she and Yaniya were best friends and had grown up together. Neither one of us could figure out why she would do such a shady thing like that.

"She didn't give you a clue as to why she was doing this?" Karena tearfully asked Kima.

I knew it was hard for her to show her emotions in front of us, but it was too late to be frontin'. Something like that was bound to break down even the toughest of girls when their alleged best friend was the culprit.

"All she said, over and over again was that you'd be gettin' what you deserved. I'm so sorry that I had anything to do with this!" Kima replied.

"Well regardless of your participation, I do thank you for stepping up and being honest. I just can't believe this!"

I heard some keys jingling in the door so I hurried up and stashed myself away in Karena's bedroom closet.

"Ooh, K your place is nice," I heard Yaniya said. "I love that candy dish, is it real Crystal?"

"Yeah, Reggie's mom gave it to me as a house warming gift. I figured that just because I was at odds with her son didn't mean I had to get rid of the dish!"

"Hell naw girl, you never throw stuff like that or jewelry away when you stop dating someone."

"Speaking of dating: what's the deal with you and Ty?"

"Ty? Baby please, I canceled his ass like a bad check as soon as we got home from being down here. We had just landed at the airport when I gave him his walkin' papers."

I held in a laugh; I knew that was some bullshit!

Karena showed Yaniya around the apartment and I prayed that she remembered my hiding space and wouldn't let her look in her closets! I exhaled thankfully when I heard Yaniya ask to listen to some music and they left the room.

"Come on; let's get something started up in here! We need to be celebrating the fact that you got rid of that no class havin', pour excuse of a boyfriend, cheatin' ass jailbird! Do you have anything to drink and I mean something with some alcohol?"

"Niya relax; there'll be plenty of time for partying later. I want you to listen to this first."

"Well it better be something lively 'cause you know I hate to be bored!" Yaniya said.

"Oh I'm sure you'll find it interesting."

That was my cue! I eased out of the closet and appeared in the living room just as Karena began playing the tape.

"What's he doing here?" Yaniya snapped when she saw me.

"Never mind me; you're attention needs to be tuned in to that tape," I pointed.

Yaniya's expression changed as she listened to herself making a deal with Kima.

"If you agree to meet up with me I'll answer all of your questions and explain the proposition I have for you."

I walked over and stood behind Karena, presenting our united front against Yaniya.

"K, what the fuck is going here? Who's that supposed to be on that tape?" She asked.

Right on point the recorded voice said, *"My name is Chi Chi…"*

Karena stopped the tape.

"Chi Chi, remember?" Karena asked her. "That's what your mother used to call you when you were a baby because she joked that you came out lookin' like one of those Munchichies, from the old cartoon."

Silence.

"Why Niya, why would you of all people wanna play me like this?"

Yaniya still said nothing.

"You had spent all your money payin' Kima off, that's why your phone was disconnected and you were staying with your dad; you couldn't afford to pay your bills."

Yaniya shifted nervously.

"Tell me why gatdammit! You owe me that much at least!"

"I don't owe you shit!" Yaniya lashed out. "Little Miss perfect; always had it all. Always threw up in my face what I didn't have: Your perfect little family with all your perfect little outings and bonding and shit!"

So that's what this was all about; Yaniya was jealous!

"My family and I always included you, Niya! We always treated you like you were a part of the family!"

"Bullshit! You loved it didn't you: the fact that my mother didn't give a rat's fat ass about me and left me by myself all the damn time? You loved flauntin' all your shit in my face, even your decision to come here! All you did was talk about leaving and you didn't once ask me to come with you!"

Karena was feeling weak but she needed to stand her ground. I massaged her shoulders and encouraged her to continue what she'd set out to do.

"Come on baby; don't let her get to you," I said.

I guess it was my turn to get the brunt of Yaniya's wrath because she hissed at me, "And you need to stay the fuck up outta it; this doesn't concern you! You would've cheated on her anyway! I saw the way you were flirtin' with Kima; you wanted to fuck her!"

"You don't know nothin' about me, little girl!" I shot back.

"I know everything was cool before she met you! There was still a chance that she would've asked me to move down here with her if she had of never met your fresh-outta-prison ass!"

Suddenly Yaniya grabbed Karena and hugged her.

"I'm sorry K. I just wanted you to come home! There was nobody for me to turn to once you left. None of this would've happened if you had of just asked me to come with you. All you had to do was ask me!"

Karena pushed her away.

"You're sick! You need some serious help, Yaniya."

"There ain't shit wrong with me!"

"I want you outta my house and outta my life!" Karena choked out.

Yaniya lost her badass demeanor and whined, "You don't mean that, K; we're best friends, remember?"

"We used to be. But then again I guess we were never really friends at all. Now get the hell out!"

"Where am I supposed to go?"

"Take a cab to the bus station and take your ass back to Ohio!"

Epilogue

The church was beautifully decorated with blue and white flowers and crepe paper and the guests were filing in. My cousin Billy was an excellent pianist and softly played classical medleys on the baby grand as the ushers showed people to their seats.

It was our wedding day: mine and Reggie's.

I was hidden away in the basement of the church I had grown up in and was being fussed over by several of my aunts and older cousins. I was a bit flushed, not because I was nervous but because there was so many people all over me messing with my hair and make-up and smoothing any unforeseen wrinkles in my hand-beaded satin dress.

My mother managed to break through the crowd of women and placed my tiara-like veil on

top of my braids, which were neatly pulled back
into a bun with a few tresses hanging down.

"How are you feeling, baby?" My mom
asked me. "Are you nervous?"

"No, I'm fine. I just wanna get up there and
marry that man!" I told her.

Amari rushed in and shouted, "It's time
ladies!"

It seemed like a thousand congratulations
were offered to me before everyone scattered off.
My father brushed past the anxious women and
kissed me on the cheek.

"You look beautiful," He told me.

"Thank you, Daddy." We hugged and he
walked me up to the sanctuary.

We waited at the double doors for the music
to start. When the beginning notes to Etta James'

"At Last" began to play, the doors opened

gracefully and we started my processional. My

eyes fixed on Reggie and it was as if we were the

only two people in the completely crowded church.

We were soul mates; I believed that with

every fiber of my being.

Reggie's white tuxedo brought out the

radiance in his Hershey's-like skin and his diamond

cufflinks sparkled brightly.

He flashed his million-dollar smile at me

and mouthed, "I love you" and I did the same.

As I scanned the row of bridesmaids, Niya's

absence appeared clear to me. I never imagined that

she would not be here to share this day with me. I

thought about the promises we made to each other

when we were kids: We would be in each other's

wedding, we would have kids together, and we would be next-door neighbors.

It's a trip because as much as she had hurt me I realized that it was for my own good in the end. Even though I had lost Niya and our friendship, I had found something that much more special in my love for Reggie. In my opinion, it was just all a part of going through the motions.